HARVEY MADDEN

by

Doug McKim

SAME OLD STORY PUBLISHING

VICTOR FERUS, President and CEO

This novel is suitable for high school teens, college students, parents and educators. It touches upon themes shared by time-less classics as 'To Kill a Mockingbird' and 'Catcher in the Rye',

This novel should be made available for confused, conflicted, and at-risk youth.

Front cover artwork by Richard McKim
Doug McKim Photo by Aaron Milner Photography

"A love letter to the state of Oregon, a heartfelt slice-of-life, love, and acceptance, which doesn't flinch from the harsh realities of the world."

Robert Midgett, author of

VAGABONDS and PRAXIS

HARVEY MADDEN

"Bury Me Not on the Lone Prairie" Adapted from 'The Ocean Burial' by Edwin Hubbell Chapin and George N. Allen.

"Beautiful Dreamer" by Stephen Foster

"In the Pines" (Traditional)

"Streets of Laredo" Derived by 'The Unfortunate Rake' (Traditional)

"I'm a Good Ol' Rebel" by James Innes Randolph

"Dixie" by Daniel D. Emmett

"Battle Hymn of the Republic" by Julia Ward Howe

"Battle Cry of Freedom" by George Frederick Root

"Jole Blon" (Cajun Traditional)

"Amazing Grace" by E. O. Excell and John Newton

"House of the Rising Sun" by Allen Price (Traditional)

"Barbara Allen" (Traditional)

"Abide With Me" by Henry Francis Lyte

"Greensleeves" (Traditional)

"Auld Lang Syne" by Robert Burns (Traditional)

Halfway Oregon is a small town in an area referred to as the Panhandle of Baker County. It's a short drive west of the Snake River, not far from the Oregon-Idaho border. It has a population of three-to-four hundred people, and sits at an elevation of about twenty-six-hundred feet above sea level.

The town's name derived from a need to place a post office "halfway" between a village known as Pine Town and a once-thriving mining community of Cornucopia. It's also near the 45th Parallel .... Halfway between the North Pole and the Equator.

Halfway was incorporated in 1909.

While certain places mentioned in HARVEY MADDEN do exist, others are inventions of the author's imagination, or thinly disguised depictions of locations and businesses where names were changed to avoid disputes, hurt feelings, or (God-forbid) legal actions. My version of Halfway may not necessarily resemble the views of others. It was my intent to capture the honorable characteristics of Halfway in its kindness, generosity, willingness to help others in a time of need, and eagerness to welcome strangers. I truly hope I've recreated Halfway in a positive light.

I've also taken a few liberties to play fast and loose with other elements of Oregon history, culture, and geography. I did this for the sake of dramatic license .... Or simply because I felt like it!

DM

Dedicated to my sister Harriet, who was my greatest supporter and fan. I only wish she was here to read this newest story.

Many thanks to my cousin, Phil Hensley, for sharing his stories and insights on the life of musicians. And appreciation to Chance Lovell, for his knowledge and advice on the world of trap shooting. Without Phil or Chance, this book would not have been possible.

1

"'Oh, I'm a good ol' rebel, Now, that's just what I am' ...'"

It was a hot as hell August day. Billy Joe McBain worked like hell doing a job that most associates at Big W believed was hell. But instead of regarding it as hell, Billy Joe simply figured, "Oh, what the hell?" then really gave it hell.

Billy Joe was a stockman at the Big W Super Center in Inland City, Oregon. His work involved pushing shopping carts into the cart bays near the front end of the giant retailer. He also carried groceries and other goods to peoples' cars. He occasionally emptied and performed minor maintenance upon the beverage container recycle machines near the store's grocery-side entrance.

Very few people wanted to be a stockman. The work was sweaty and strenuous. It was near the bottom rung of the ladder, in terms of status and pay. Most stockmen hated their place in the political structure of Big W ... everyone but Billy Joe. He handled the job of stockman as a form of discipline, athleticism, and virtue. He took pride in physical labor. Billy Joe possessed a grace, skill, and beauty in handling carts, which he easily maneuvered through a maze of automobiles and lampposts through the parking lot. He enjoyed working outside where the air was fresh and the scenery beautiful despite the changing of seasons and weather. He was quick on his feet, and outworked his fellow stockmen without complaint.

Billy Joe McBain was seventeen, and an upcoming senior at Grangeford High. He was six feet tall, with a thin yet sinewy physique. He was the son of an Irish-American father and a Mexican and Nez Percé mother. He had narrow, piercing blue eyes, straight black hair trimmed neatly above the ears and neck, and a dark complexion. He wore a black Remington Arms baseball cap, blue plaid shirt, and a green, fluorescent safety vest. His khaki cargo shorts revealed two tanned and muscular legs. He had on white ankle socks and lightweight, leather hiking shoes. Upon his upper lip was a first try at growing a mustache.

Billy Joe showed off his musical abilities by singing in a deep baritone voice. He worked tirelessly while belting out songs of life in the wide, open spaces, the isolation of being a ranch hand amongst herds of cattle, the brutality and stupidity of gun violence, freezing to death in blinding winter blizzards, or gruesome demises during frenzied stampedes.

It was a scorching afternoon, with temperatures above ninety. The only relief came from a constant breeze. Inland was a small town of about two-thousand people, adjacent to its larger sister community of Grangeford. Both cities were nestled within a high-mountain desert nearly three-thousand feet above sea level, surrounded by rolling hills and granite peaks of the Wallowa Mountains. It was an area of dry summer droughts, brutally cold winters, and ceaseless wind.

To the north was the familiar and comforting image of Mount Emily, which stood as a massive, earthbound goddess upholding constant visage over those living below her. Grangeford was a town of fifteen thousand people, and home of Northern Oregon University, one of two state colleges east of the Cascade Range.

"Carry out on Aisle One," a tinny voice requested from a small, walkie-talkie clipped to Billy Joe's belt.

"On my way," replied Billy Joe, while pushing a string of twelve carts into the bay near the general merchandise doors. He then entered a large, air-conditioned store. He smiled and tipped his cap to customers while strolling toward Aisle One where a sixty-five-inch TV, sitting upon an L-cart, awaited him.

The cashier who sold the TV was Billy Joe's closest companion, Harvey Madden.

Harvey was a lad of sixteen, with long, blonde hair hanging below a pair of scrawny shoulders. He stood only five-five, and had a fair complexion. He wore a bright yellow, Big W vest, a red and white jersey with three-quarter length sleeves, blue jean shorts, and sneakers.

"Billy Joe's here to help you," informed Harvey, introducing the young stockman to an elderly couple. "He'll be more than happy to give you a hand with your TV."

"Aw, just call me 'Cheyenne'," greeted Billy Joe. He bowed at the older couple and proudly ran one finger along his mustache.

The elderly couple snickered as Harvey merely rolled his eyes back and sighed.

Billy Joe pushed the L-cart to a mid sized Toyota Tacoma parked in a handicapped zone. There, he helped the husband place the TV into the back of their vehicle. The elderly couple happily offered Billy Joe ten dollars for assisting them.

"It's a'right," responded Billy Joe. "Store policy won't let me accept it."

"Take it," the husband insisted, slapping the money in Billy Joe's hand. "Couldn't o' got that monstrosity in our car without ya!"

Customers often sought to give Billy Joe a gratuity. Although it made Billy Joe feel valued and appreciated, Big W was firm in their ruling that associated were not to take money or gifts from customers. "Honest, folks," answered Billy Joe. "Wish I could take it, but it'll be my hide if ..."

"What your bosses don't know won't hurt 'em," the husband said, grinning mischievously. "Take it before I shove it where the sun don't shine!"

Billy Joe bid the couple a good afternoon. He reentered the store and gave the ten dollars to a customer service manager. By now, the time was nearly four in the afternoon, when Billy Joe could clock out and prepare for a three-day weekend in the mountains near the village of Halfway.

Billy Joe went to the recycle center to hang up his safety vest.

The recycle center was where plastic bottles, aluminum cans, and glass containers were crushed by machines, then placed into bins. Those using the machines were compensated a dime for each accepted container. The recycle center, or "bottle room", was harsh, claustrophobic, and smelly. There were no windows to let in air or sunlight. The walls were a dull, white sheetrock, and floors forged of concrete. Bins filled with crushed cans and bottles were taken to a "can cage", behind Big W.

The bottle room was ruled over by a brawny, middle-aged man named Mitch, who figured he owned the place and everything in it, including the Envipco machines which crushed and bagged containers. Mitch had round, steel-framed glasses and a thick black mustache which Billy Joe was jealous of because it resembled the facial hair worn by Wyatt Earp.

"Hope you have a swell weekend," said Billy Joe, giving Mitch a snotty grin.

"I wish you idiot stockmen weren't allowed in here while I'm working!" groaned Mitch. He viewed others with contempt, and remained none-too-friendly.

"You ain't working," commented Billy Joe. "I never seen you do an honest day's work since I been here. Hell, you're always in hiding from management in here."

Billy Joe giggled, did an about-face, and left the recycle center on his way to the break room.

"Faggot," Mitch mumbled under his breath. "Goddamn loudmouthed faggot…"

*****

Big W's associate break room was furnished with a half-dozen round tables, a bar, refrigerator, microwave oven, coffee pot, big-screen TV, and a couch. It was an area where associates hung out, enjoyed meals and simple conversation, and relaxed.

Harvey sat in the room with an older, part-time cashier named Di, and a self-service cashier known as Shelby Newton.

Shelby was twenty-three. He was a nervous, antsy, fidgety sort. He wore a long-sleeved, turtleneck sweater, to conceal the self-inflicted scars on his wrists and arms. He had on a pair of corduroy shorts, black socks, and Hush Puppies. He spoke with a noticeable, high-pitched lisp. He rarely said a word, yet remained extremely polite.

While he did fairly well for himself at Big W, Shelby was considered a wimp, a wussy, a pansy, a sissy … and a queer.

Shelby had recently been hospitalized for a suicide attempt, due to the ceaseless bigotry and prejudices ranged against him. He was quiet, and seemingly resided within the shadows. Harvey respected Shelby as a friend and a coworker, yet also felt sorry for him. He feared ending up like Shelby, a marginalized, misunderstood, and ill-treated soul.

Di had worked at the Inland City Big W since it first opened in 1993. She was a heavy-set woman with gray hair rolled in a bun, bright blue eyes, a round face and a double-chin.

Harvey sat at with Di, nibbling on an Idaho Spud candy bar.

"Ready for your long weekend?" Di asked him.

Harvey simply nodded.

"Does your folks know about you and Billy Joe?" whispered Di.

Harvey responded with a fiery blush, a tightened throat, and a nervous giggle.

"I've known your folks since before you were born," stated Di, sympathetically. "Believe me, Harve. They'll be fine with it."

Harvey pasted on a lopsided grin and shot an anxious glance at Shelby Newton.

Billy Joe entered the break room and smiled once he saw Harvey waiting there for him. Harvey stood to greet Billy Joe, who answered by kissing him on the forehead. "Ready to go?" asked Billy Joe.

Harvey was equally flattered and embarrassed by the smooch. He bit his bottom lip as a tear slipped from one eye.

"You boys have a wonderful time!" cheered Di. "Tell me all about it when you get back!"

"No worries," spoke Billy Joe, one arm around Harvey's shoulders. "We're gonna have a helluva good time! Ain't we, Harve?"

Harvey shrugged. "I guess," he said, his voice barely audible. He feigned a calm demeanor, gave Di a wave, and mouthed goodbye.

He then left the break room, for his three-day weekend with Billy Joe McBain.

2

Harvey and Billy Joe stepped outside and headed toward the associates' parking spot, not far from a nearby mini mall featuring Cellular One, Verizon, Taco Time, and a few taverns and diners. The asphalt surface of the parking lot was hot enough to fry eggs and bacon on.

The two teens went to Billy Joe's red, '95 GMC Sierra pickup. The GMC featured a standard cab, automatic transmission, black, leather upholstery and a gun rack in the back window. CDs and hunting magazines covered the seat. Harvey and Billy Joe hopped inside. Both windows had been left shut, and the GMC's interior resembled an oven.

Harvey and Billy Joe rolled down their windows to let fresh air sweep in. Billy Joe fired up the ignition, and turned the air conditioning up. He exchanged his baseball cap for a black Stetson cowboy hat. He scrounged through a number of CDs and found a personal favorite which he played over and over again. It was a greatest hits collection from Bob Wills and His Texas Playboys, noted musicians throughout the Thirties, Forties, and Fifties.

Billy Joe placed the CD in the GMC's sound system, tuned the volume up, and let everyone within range hear 'San Antonio Rose'. He glanced in the rearview mirror to admire himself, then sped out of the parking lot while the music played loud enough to wake the dead. The GMC roared along Inland Avenue toward Grangeford.

"I'm getting sick and tired of getting sick and tired of Bob Wills," groaned Harvey, rolling his eyes back and sighing. "How come you never play the newer country?"

"I'd rather listen to the pioneers of country and western. Gospel, folk, bluegrass, Western Swing, honky-tonk ... y' know. I'm wanna learn from them who came first. Them who made country popular in the first place."

Harvey frowned. "This was popular?"

"Sure as shit was," laughed Billy Joe. "At the time."

"Yeah, but is it now?"

Billy Joe shrugged. "Aw, hell, I dunno. Some folks still like it. I sure do."

"Well, I don't," commented Harvey. "I can't stand how that guy keeps cutting in with his stupid, high-pitched 'ah-ha!' 'Yeah!' 'All together now!' 'Domino!' and all that other stupid crap."

"The guy you're harping about was Bob Wills," explained Billy Joe, continuing to admire himself in the rearview mirror.

Harvey shook his head. "So, why'd he make all that damn noise for?"

"Aw, just his way of doing things, I reckon."

"Well, I don't like it."

"A'right, so you don't like my music," countered Billy Joe. "What about all them old books you got?"

"What're you talking about?"

"'Conan,' 'Tarzan,' 'John Carter', 'Sherlock Holmes', 'Huckleberry Finn', 'The Last of the Mohicans'. They're old, ain't they?"

"But I wanna be a writer!" argued Harvey. "I learn by reading old books!"

"And I'm gonna be a musician. That's why I listen to old music ... all them dead guys you don't like. You learn from dead writers, and I learn from dead singers."

Billy Joe dreamed of being a musician. Harvey wished to write imaginative fiction ... fantasy, sci-fi, horror. Harvey never cared for Billy Joe's music. Chances were, Billy Joe never liked Harvey's literature, if he even bothered with it!

Harvey lived in the neighborhood which was referred to as Snob Hill, at the southwestern section of Grangeford near a hospital. It featured narrow avenues and boulevards which carried the names of US Presidents. Harvey lived on the corner of Cherry and Roosevelt, in a white, two-story house built more than a century ago. A couple of Tamaracks and one fir tree towered over the front lawn. The backyard had a spacious swimming pool and a concrete wall for privacy.

Harvey was the last of five children, born when his parents were nearly fifty. His four siblings had already left the nest before he came into the world. The eldest, Danny, lived across town with his wife and three children. Two of his kids were nearly Harvey's age, yet called him "uncle". The second, Sherry, resided in Rhode Island. The third, Eli, currently stayed at an alcohol and drug rehab in Kansas City. The fourth, Carson, had married an Asian woman and taught at a university in Hong Kong.

Terry and Elaine Madden were in their mid-sixties. Terry worked part-time designing and constructing homes made of mud, steel beams, mesh wire, and fifty-pound, rectangular hay bales.

Terry and Elaine maintained a youthful vigor. They enjoyed a mainly vegan diet, and went for long walks. They often wore shorts, and took pride in their muscular frames and tanned bodies. Terry allowed his gray hair and beard to grow long and shaggy, the way he wore it in his teens and twenties. He was a moderate marijuana smoker, and his study smelled of it.

Although it was freely offered to him, Harvey never used pot.

While Terry and Elaine granted him more liberty than most kids dreamed of, Harvey never gave himself the freedom to reveal his love of Billy Joe. He'd been dating Billy Joe for several months, and twice engaged in sex. Even if a few people knew that Harvey and Billy Joe were a "couple", no one told Terry and Elaine. This was on Harvey's mind when he and Billy Joe entered his home overlooking Grangeford.

Harvey and Billy Joe found Terry and Elaine sitting on lawn chairs in the backyard, listening to Neil Diamond and drinking bottles of a regional brew known as Terminal Gravity. Harvey rushed upstairs to take a shower in the bathroom adjacent to his own quarters, at the end of a hallway.

Once he cleaned up, Harvey put on a thin, white tee-shirt, cut-off jeans, and worn-out Converses. As he collected his camping gear, he heard Terry and Billy Joe arguing politics.

"I'm not in the market of buying your right-wing bullshit today," said Terry, offering Billy Joe a cold beer. "And I won't take an interest in it tomorrow."

"Ain't gonna be here tomorrow," responded Billy Joe. "I'm kidnapping your youngest brat and hauling his ass with me into the woods tonight. I'll hold 'em ransom over the weekend, unless I get sick of his belly-achin' and whining."

"I got a better idea," said Terry. "Drop by later this evening and I'll convince you to become a Democrat."

"Only if you accept one of my 'Make America Great Again' hats."

"You would support that Nazi bastard, wouldn't ya?"

"Like the true red, white, and blue American which I am, and always will be," snickered Billy Joe. "Better to be red, white, and blue than a stinking Red like you."

"You keep talking like that," threatened Terry, jokingly, "I'm gonna kick your ass so hard it'll be red, white, and blue for a month. Sit down, shut up, and drink up!"

Billy Joe sat at a lawn chair and took a swig.

As Harvey wandered downstairs, Elaine got up from her lawn chair and called him into the kitchen.

Elaine Madden kept her hair slightly below the shoulders. She dyed it dark brown in hopes of concealing her age. She wore a thin, white blouse, a pair of shorts and leather sandals. Though she frequented a local gym, Elaine still had a bit of a tummy which embarrassed her.

As both sat at the table, Elaine placed Harvey's hand in hers. "Are you and Billy Joe gonna be okay in the mountains, alone?" she asked in concern.

"Don't worry," answered Harvey. "We'll be fine."

"You two are really close," whispered Elaine glancing outside at Billy Joe. "Aren't you?"

Harvey said nothing, yet wondered where this conversation was going. Did Elaine know of his true feelings for Billy Joe? Was this her way of tip-toeing to the point? Harvey fought back a blush and struggled not to look ashamed or guilty.

"I know it hasn't been easy not having Danny, Carson, or Eli around," Elaine went on. "It's nice that Billy Joe's been like a brother to you."

"So am I," sighed Harvey. "He is my best friend and my big brother, Mom."

"I haven't always liked some of the kids you've brought over here, Harve. But neither Terry or I have a problem with Billy Joe. Nor do we have trouble inviting him over, day or night. And I know ..." Elaine swallowed. "I hope ... that the two of you will stay safe ... You ... You two will stay safe ... Won't you?"

"Trust me," chuckled Harvey. "Nothing will happen to us while ..."

"Don'tcha think it's time for us to head out, hombre?" interrupted Billy Joe, strutting into the kitchen like he owned it. "I wanna get the tent set-up before nightfall, so bears and Bigfoot won't mosey along and eat us."

Harvey released a high-pitched giggle.

"Aw, don't you fret none," Billy Joe told Elaine. "Your little Harve's got three guys looking after him."

"'Three guys'?" questioned Elaine, nervously.

"Smith, Wesson ..." said Billy Joe, in a lousy Clint Eastwood impersonation. "And me ..."

Harvey jumped to his feet, said his goodbyes to Terry and Elaine, then rushed outside with Billy Joe.

"Be careful, son!" Elaine's voice echoed through the house, as Harvey shut the front door behind him. "Please, Harvey? ... You will be careful, won't you? ... Harvey? Please stay safe, won't you? Please? ..."

3

Billy Joe thought his little joke was hilarious. He knew exactly which buttons to throw Elaine into a panic, and habitually pushed them.

In truth, Elaine worried as much about Billy Joe as she did for Harvey. She regarded Billy Joe as a sibling to Harvey, as much as Danny, Eli, or Carson. Regrettably, Harvey rarely had a chance to see Eli or Carson. One lived on the other side of the world, while the other never stayed out of trouble. Both rarely made it home to eastern Oregon. Although Danny only lived a few blocks away, he gave little time for Harvey. Between Little League, soccer, ballet, late-afternoons at the golf course, and his accounting firm, Danny's days were filled.

Harvey and Billy Joe began their trip toward Halfway, roughly a hundred miles to the northeast. Billy Joe fastened his seat belt, turned the ignition, took a moment to primp in the rearview mirror, then scrounged through a pile of CDs for tunes to make the journey more agreeable, at least for him. Billy Joe found a compilation of noted Italian western film scores from Ennio Morricone. He turned the volume up full blast, and made sure everyone in town heard it.

As the GMC cruised into Main Street, Grangeford got a taste of music from 'A Fistful of Dollars', 'The Good, the Bad, and the Ugly', and 'Once Upon a Time in the West'. Billy Joe smiled wickedly, knowing that he turned heads and caught attention. Meanwhile, Harvey struggled yet failed to be invisible.

Within a few minutes, the GMC passed the local Bi-Mart, a couple of beer and soda pop distributors, then turned onto the Old Highway 30 toward the small town of Union.

Minutes later, Billy Joe pulled into a long driveway to a ranch house where he lived with his grandparents. The property entrance featured an arched, iron gate, shaped in the image of a flintlock rifle and the name McBain. A double-wide mobile home sat in front of an aging, two-story Victorian house and a bright, red barn which housed alfalfa, chickens, goats, a burro, and a John Deere tractor.

The Chevy truck which his grandfather owned, along with Grandma Abigail's Kia, were nowhere to be seen. Abigail was gone playing bridge with her pals at a senior center, while Grandpa Fred helped a buddy swath and bail hay.

Harvey and Billy Joe entered the double-wide, to find it empty for the exception of a Norwegian Elkhound named Patty and a bluetick hound known as Corky.

There was no love between Harvey and Corky. This was demonstrated soon after Harvey stepped into the house with Billy Joe. Initially, Corky approached Billy Joe, tail wagging while he practically knocked him over in love and affection. The moment he spotted Harvey, his mood went from being warm and jovial to that of extreme anger and hostility. The hair on the back of Corky's hair bristled. Teeth bared, eyes widened in hatred and contempt. What began as low growls and snarling soon evolved into loud, shrill barks and howling.

Harvey stepped backward and nearly tripped over a brown leather couch.

"Simmer down, Corky," ordered Billy Joe, in a comical tone. "No worries, Harve. His bark's a lot worse'n his bite."

"You sure about that?" questioned Harvey. He carefully sat upon the couch and lifted both feet above the floor. "Your asshole dog wants me for dinner!"

"Aw, he just don't know you all that well yet," said Billy Joe, pulling Corky away by the collar. "He'll be fine once he gets more familiar with ya."

"I'm pretty sure I don't want to get that familiar with him!"

"Aw, c'mon. By the end of this weekend, he'll get over hating your guts, and decide to be friends."

"This weekend?"

"Yeah," Billy Joe laughed. "He's coming with us."

"Like hell he is!" shouted Harvey. "If he's coming with us, then I'm going home!"

"What for?"

"Well, can'tcha see? Your dog don't like me, and I don't like him either!"

"Give it time," said Billy Joe, entering a bedroom. "You guys'll be the best of buds in no time!"

"I doubt it," answered Harvey, suffering from a racing heart, shortness of breath, and overwhelming panic. Anytime he dared to show any affection for Billy Joe ... be it in a slap on the back, a hug, or a kiss, Corky went ballistic. Harvey suspected that Corky would eventually win out by killing him and forever ending the conflict between them.

Harvey found the McBain living room a welcoming environment ... providing that Corky wasn't there. Wood paneling, cut from a local sawmill, covered the four walls. Layers of clear stain maintained its natural color and pleasant tone. A large, spacious window to the west gave visitors a panoramic view of the farmland which the McBains owned. Black and white photos of Grandpa Fred's forefathers spoke of the family's origins in Oklahoma, Arkansas, and Missouri. Shelves of hardcover and paperback novels by Louis L'Amour, Max Brand, and Zane Grey filled an entire wall. Another shelf held a vast library of country music CDs and western DVDs. A large, wooden sign above a thirty-two-inch TV read a noted line from the film 'Ride the High Country';

"All I want is to enter my house justified."

Abigail McBain had made tuna sandwiches and left them in the refrigerator for Harvey and Billy Joe. The sandwiches were grudgingly accepted. The two teens knew from experience that tuna soon grew disgusting and gross.

Billy Joe placed the sandwiches into a cooler with other food items. He fetched a banjo, a guitar, and changes of clothes from his bedroom. Finally, he went to his grandparents' bedroom, where a gun cabinet sat in one corner.

Only Billy Joe and Grandpa Fred had keys to the gun cabinet. Fred granted Billy Joe permission to take a Ruger 12-gauge shotgun, a Remington 30.06, and a .22 revolver.

Billy Joe shaved, then got into a pair of faded Levis and a blue, plaid shirt. Before leaving his own bedroom, he glanced at a wrinkled, faded color photograph hanging from the wall above his dresser. It was a picture of Billy Joe's mother, Laci Jo McBain ... A woman he sorely missed ... a woman who lived only in dreams and memories.

Billy Joe was not yet born when the photo was taken. Laci Jo was only seventeen at the time, and stood a mere four-nine. She was of Nez Percé and Mexican descent. Her bright, brown eyes and enthusiastic, toothy grin displayed hopes for a comfortable and happy future ... A future which had somehow eluded her.

Laci Jo had dropped out of school when she wed a fellow named Steve McBain. It proved to be a short-lived marriage. One early morning, Steve went to work in the kill room of Hills Meats and never returned.

Billy Joe had spent his first six years at the Umatilla Indian Reservation near Pendleton Oregon. Laci Jo struggled to make ends meet at Wildhorse Casino, along I-84. She did her very best to raise Billy Joe on her own. Regrettably, she wasn't without her personal demons.

Those very demons had gotten the best of Laci Jo when she was found dead with a needle in her arm, at the kitchen of a modest trailer.

Billy Joe then went to live with his paternal grandparents, Fred and Abigail, on a small spread near Union. There, he helped raise chickens, rabbits, goats, ducks, geese, and a burro. Fred had instilled a love of hunting, fishing, and firearms. Billy Joe was fed on classic western movies and TV shows, along with early "hillbilly" music of the Carter Family, Jimmie Rodgers, Hank Williams, and the Sons of the Pioneers. He taught himself banjo and guitar.

Billy Joe never knew his father, Steve, who spent more time behind bars than working steady employment or offering financial assistance to his only child.

Billy Joe fought back tears as he examined Laci Jo's photo. It was easier to concentrate on the three days he'd spend with Harvey in the mountains and of the life he now had, instead of a what might have been.

***

Harvey, Billy Joe, and Corky hopped into the GMC and raced out of the driveway.

Billy Joe listened to his Spaghetti Western CD, and admired himself in the rearview mirror. Harvey hated Billy Joe's mustache. It didn't make him look dashing, daring, suave, charming, debonair, or roguish. Nor did he appear as an adult with it. Instead, Billy Joe came off as a little boy, trying to wear grown-up men's clothing which never fit.

The GMC passed a long row of towering wind turbines spanning across the flatlands and rolling hills of a high mountain desert.

"Billy Joe," Harvey asked, with uncertainty. "Do you think? ... You think I'm a good cashier?"

"The best," claimed Billy Joe.

Harvey's voice quivered. "What makes you say that?"

"Aw, you do a real thankless job. Probably the most thankless job in the whole store."

"Even more 'thankless' than pushing carts?"

"I got my freedom outside, Harve. Long as I do my job, they pretty much leave me alone. You got the public to deal with. You paste on a shit-eating grin and play nice to ornery people. You work harder'n all them other cashiers combined!" Billy Joe slapped Harvey's leg, while Corky responded with a snarl.

"Thanks," whispered Harvey.

"I reckon we'll do real good once we leave Big W and get on with our lives. You'll head off to college somewhere, while I spend a few years in the Army. Pretty soon we'll both head to Nashville where I'll make it big as a folk and country singer, and you'll make it big as a writer."

Harvey rolled his eyes back and sighed. No matter how much he loathed Billy Joe's stupid mustache, he dreaded thoughts of his boyfriend in the military. Terry and Elaine protested any and all interventions that the United States involved itself in, since Iraq in the early 90s. Terry even spent time in jail for taking part in an anti-war march which led to a riot.

Harvey didn't have to voice his opposition to Billy Joe's plans of enlisting in the Army. His sad eyes and gritting teeth said more than words ever could.

"Aw, you got nothing to worry about," laughed Billy Joe. "I won't get myself killed. Bet your bottom dollar on that!"

"I love you," mouthed Harvey, in a plea. He reached out to touch Billy Joe's shoulder. Corky bristled up, bared his teeth, and barked.

Harvey quickly pulled his hand back.

"Corky," scolded Billy Joe, tiredly. "Look, it don't matter where I am or what I'm doing, as long as we're together. I love ya too, Harve. And I promise to be loyal while I'm off serving our country. Trust me, I ain't getting mixed up with someone else."

"I hope not," spoke Harvey, his insides tied in knots.

"Reckon you ain't gonna fool around behind my back while I'm off in some nasty third-world shithole for Uncle Sam."

"Hell, no! What makes you think I'd? ..."

"I know you better'n that." Billy Joe smiled. "But, look it. You don't gotta worry about me, a'right? Nothing bad's gonna happen. I'll do my time in the Army, save up some money for a down payment on a nice place, just for the two of us. Then I promise never to leave you again for anybody or anything! A'right?"

Silence.

"A'right?" pressed Billy Joe.

"Yeah, okay," breathed Harvey. "I just wanna make sure nothing happens to ya ... That's all ..."

"Billy Joe laughed. "I swear, Harve! Sometimes you carry on worse than your mother does!"

Harvey gritted his teeth, then gave Billy Joe a menacing glare. Too angry to speak, he turned his head away and stared blankly outside for several minutes.

4

The trip remained quiet, for the exception of the music which played loudly over the stereo.

Harvey didn't mind Ennio Morricone so much, and occasionally wrote while listening to the scores of 'Once Upon a Time in America' and 'Cinema Paradiso'. That moment, he concentrated on the distant image of the Elkhorn Mountains along the southern horizon. The Elkhorns were rough, rugged, brutally harsh and breathtakingly beautiful. Grand, snow-covered peaks that resembled physical, earthbound gods, imposing and unshaking in their mere presence. The mountain range stood several thousand feet above the valley floor.

Along with the Wallowas, the Elkhorn Mountains were known as the Alps of North America.

Northeastern Oregon attracted hunters, hikers, skiers, fishermen, photographers, snowmobilers, and other tourists. For Harvey, it was fodder for the myths and tall tales conjured in his imagination. He visualized great cities lost within the mountain passes and canyons, along with various races and wild beasts residing there. Harvey's thoughts held stories of quests and conquests, heroic fables of victory and tragedy, usually dealing with young male protagonists who prove their courage and therefore earn the right to become leaders of their tribe. He visualized large castles and fortresses, built of stone and steel, impenetrable in their sheer scale and grandeur, defended by wit, strategy, skill, and bravery. In his stories, even the finest heroes may meet terrible ends, to be avenged by those of equal or greater abilities. Yet, they'd be remembered in written scrolls and vocal accounts, told around campfires.

The GMC rolled through North Powder, on the Union/Baker County line. North Powder was a town of about two-thousand people. After passing a few businesses and service stations, Billy Joe was about to make a left onto eastbound Interstate 84 when he noticed a lone figure begging for a ride.

The hitcher was likely not a day older than Harvey or Billy Joe. He was a skinny teen with a thin build and a sad, waif-like face under unruly brown hair. He was dressed in a baggy, blue sweatshirt, khaki shorts, worn out sneakers and dirty, white ankle socks.

The hitcher pointed his thumb toward Baker City and waved frantically at Harvey, Billy Joe, and an ornery hound dog.

Harvey glanced at Billy Joe. "Think we oughta give him a lift?"

Billy Joe replied with an assuring grin. He pulled the GMC to one side and stopped.

The hitcher happily fetched a back pack and sleeping bag sitting upon the ground next to him. He tossed them in the back, then dashed to the passenger side where Harvey was. "Catch a ride?" he asked.

"Sure!" urged Billy Joe. "Hop in!"

Despite Corky's objections, Harvey slid toward Billy Joe to make room.

The hitcher introduced himself as Nick Fredericks from Stanfield.

Harvey and Billy Joe gave their names. "Just call me 'Cheyenne'," added Billy Joe, once more admiring himself in the rearview mirror. "Where ya heading?"

"Away from where I'm leaving," sighed Nick.

"We can get you as far as Baker City," informed Billy Joe. "Me and Harve are on our way to Halfway."

"Cool," said Nick, glancing all around the GMC's cab. "Mind ... Mind if I ask you guys ... a personal question?"

"What?" asked Harvey, pleasantly.

"You ... you been smoking weed in here?" asked Nick.

Harvey's grin quickly faded as he shook his head in denial. "Why?... What makes you think?" he muttered, his voice high-pitched and panicky.

"Not tryna put you on the spot," mumbled Nick." Just that ... It smells like marijuana in here. No ... No big deal, really. Just kinda wondering, that's all."

Harvey rolled his eyes back and sighed.

Billy Joe giggled and Corky growled.

"My ... It's my parents," stuttered Harvey, self-consciously. "My ... My parents ... they smoke it all the time. Guess the smell got into my clothes ... I ... I guess ..."

"If you say so," Nick commented, wickedly. "Whatever you say, pal. It's all good by me."

Harvey searched for a way to explain that he never used marijuana. What was the use? Hoping to change the subject, he fetched a box of Western Family chocolate chip granola bars, and handed them to Nick.

"Munchies!" snickered Nick, graciously accepting the snack.

"Any idea where you're going?" asked Harvey, struggling to regain his composure.

"No clue," answered Nick. He came off as a frail, frightened, fragile soul, easily victimized, possibly tortured or killed if he met with the wrong company.

Harvey felt a need to protect Nick, but realized that he could not. Even then, thoughts of seeing Nick alone and vulnerable, with no one to fall back on, were unspeakable. "No clue?" questioned Harvey, sadly.

"Anywhere's better than where I've been!" spoke Nick.

"And where was that?" asked Billy Joe.

"Hell," was all Nick said. "I been to Hell, and I ain't going back."

Harvey and Billy Joe traded glances, as Corky snarled.

Once they reached Baker City, Billy Joe pulled off of the interstate to gas up. Harvey asked to go to McDonalds, so he and Nick could enjoy a meal and talk.

As Billy Joe went to a service station, Harvey and Nick stepped inside to find a boisterous and hectic afternoon at the Golden Arches. The two boys got in line, waited their turns, and ordered a couple of Big Macs and Cokes. They sat down at a booth and often glanced out at a busy Campbell Street. A half-dozen girls, most dressed in skimpy tank tops and shorts, wandered along the sidewalk. A couple of middle school boys sped by on stingray bicycles. A bright blue Dodge pickup, displaying 'Don't Tread on Me' and a Confederate flag, roared loudly. Harvey wished to speak concerning Nick's dire situation, but didn't know where to start.

"I had to get out of a mess," sobbed Nick, battling tears as both lips quivered. "I couldn't stay for any longer, unless I killed myself or somebody else!" Conscious that his voiced grew louder as he spoke, Nick thought it best to whisper. "Mom ... Mom died some time back, so she wasn't there to help me! Even if she was there, she wasn't much help ... drunk, stoned, or sober! It only got worse after she passed away!"

"What? What did?" Harvey braced himself for things which made him shutter.

"Dad's doping, boozing, him beating up on me. Just 'cause I wouldn't steal to support his habits! Him beating on me for no reason other than me being born or living and breathing!" Nick's eyes met Harvey's. "And if that lazy, fat bastard wasn't forcing me to steal for him, then he ... He whored me out to pervert buddies of his!"

Harvey's eyes widened. "But why? ... Why didn't you call the cops?"

"One of the guys who had his way with me was a cop!" shouted Nick, no longer caring who heard him. "And if it wasn't him then it was a local business owner or a preacher or an asshole social worker! Who'd take my word over theirs? I had no choice but to leave!"

Harvey sighed. He was glad that he and Billy Joe had taken Nick as far as Baker City. But, now what? Before long, Harvey and Billy Joe would make their way toward Halfway. Where did that leave Nick? Where would he go from there?

Guilt and shame swept over Harvey. He had a decent home, a cozy bed, and a warm home and a loving family. Why did he deserve such good things? And why did Nick deserve such a horrible existence? "Is there ..." started Harvey. "You got anyone to stay with? Friends or family members? Any?... Any safe place to go?"

"Like I said, I got no clue where I'm going. And as long as I'm running away from someone and someplace, I ain't safe."

"But?... Where?" Harvey looked outside to what now appeared as a hard, harsh, cruel world. He felt wiped out and exhausted. "Where are you gonna stay, tonight? I mean ... Is there anywhere you can go?"

"The park," said Nick. "If there is one."

"There is." Harvey pointed toward downtown Baker. "Not ... not far from here ... next to the library."

"Thanks." Nick looked straight into Harvey's eyes, and fought an urge to weep. "Thanks, Harve. Thanks for the lift, the grub, and the Coke. Thanks for everything you guys done for me."

Without giving it a second thought, Harvey reached into a back pocket for his wallet. He found a folded, twenty-dollar bill, and handed it to Nick.

Nick shook his head. "I can't ..."

"Take it," insisted Harvey, shoving the money into Nick's hand. "Please take it. Trust me, it'll make us both feel better."

Nick smiled, wiped his watery eyes, and finished the meal.

***

Minutes later, Harvey and Nick stepped outside into the hot afternoon sun. One kid was going northeast, the other to destinations unknown. The two stopped to give each other one last look. Both were lost in their own chaotic thoughts. "Well," mouthed Harvey, his throat tightening. "Dunno what to say, other than to wish you ... the best of luck."

With that, Harvey gave Nick a hug.

Nick threw his arms around Harvey as well, in a tight embrace. Although the two lads were barely acquainted, they prepared for what proved to be a long, painful goodbye.

"Thanks," said Nick, holding onto Harvey as close as he possibly could. "Thanks for everything."

"Take care of yourself," begged Harvey, unable to control his frail emotions. No matter. He still had to let go, and watch Nick wander away to an uncertain and potentially dangerous future. All Harvey could do was hope and pray that Nick found security and happiness in the end.

Slowly, Nick released Harvey. He gave him a weak, nervous grin, fetched his sleeping bag and back pack from sidewalk. He turned around to make his way toward Geiser-Pollman Park, where he'd likely spend the rest of the day and possibly that night.

Harvey stood motionless as he watched Nick wander away. His vision grew murky and cloudy with tears. His back and shoulders grew tense from worry, his heart saddened by the reality of it all. Harvey suffered an overwhelming sense of helplessness and hopelessness. There was nothing he could do about it.

Harvey was shaken out of his self-imposed torture by the sounds of a familiar vehicle, along with the bittersweet melody of 'Jill's Theme' from 'Once Upon a Time in the West'. A red GMC pickup drove into the McDonalds parking lot. Inside was Billy Joe, wearing an idiotic smile and his stupid mustache. Sitting next to him, forever on guard, was Corky, who despised Harvey for no good reason than because. "You gonna stand there all day?" questioned Billy Joe. "Or are we gonna mosey on to a big, beautiful lake that's waiting for us?"

Harvey took a deep breath, straightened his spine, and got into the pickup with Billy Joe and Corky,

"Where's Nick?" asked Billy Joe, rushing out of town.

Harvey simply shrugged and shook his head. "He went his way … and I'm going mine."

"He gonna be okay?" asked Billy Joe, turning eastbound onto Highway 86.

"Dunno. I sure hope. That's all we can do is hope. I bought him a burger, gave him a twenty, and sent him on his way. All I can do is … I guess is … Damn it, I don't know, Billy Joe! I really don't."

Billy Joe chuckled as he patted Harvey's knee. Softly, he caressed Harvey's thigh, then reached up to rub his face. This, to Corky's objections. "You're a good kid, Harve. Always looking out for the other guy. Reckon that's why I love ya so damn much!"

Harvey bit his lower lip and gave Billy Joe a weak smile. "Thanks," he said, barely audible over the loud music and the rumble of the GMC's engine. "Love you too, Billy Joe. I love you, too."

5

Harvey and Billy Joe passed the Oregon Trail Interpretive Center, in a region known as Virtue Flats. Ruts and relics from covered wagons were still found, examined, and studied. The area was rough, rustic, barren, harsh, lonely, and somewhat inhospitable. It consisted of sagebrush and wildlife which called the dry flatlands and rolling hills home. The Powder River Sportsmen's Club had a firing range just off the highway, where youngsters earned hunter safety cards.

Virtue Flats resembled a landscape one encountered in western novels, TV shows, and movies. It was often a gray and (in Harvey's opinion) homely piece of ground. To the north were the granite peaks of the Eagle Cap Wilderness Area, with mountain peaks nearly ten-thousand feet in altitude. Far to the east were the Idaho Rockies.

After twenty miles of alfalfa fields along with farm and ranch homes, the GMC entered a narrow, steep canyon along with the shallow, swift-moving Powder River. Midway between Baker City and Halfway was the Bishop Springs Rest Area, which was nothing more than a single, brick and concrete outhouse. Still, it was a suitable spot to stretch the legs, catch your breath, and answer a call of nature.

The Coke which Harvey sipped at McDonalds had sprinted right through him, and he desperately needed to go.

The GMC pulled off to the left, onto a dirt and gravel parking spot. An older man had just left the restroom, got into his green Buick Regal then drove toward Baker City. Harvey jumped out of the pickup, dashed into the stall, and relieved himself. Meanwhile, Billy Joe and Corky breathed in the fresh air and worked off some pent-up energy.

Minutes later, the trio got back into the GMC for the final stretch towards Halfway. Regrettably, they were unable to go anywhere, due to a recurring issue which dwelled under the GMC's hood.

"Aw, this goddamn piece of shit rig, with its goddamn piece of shit vapor lock!" cursed Billy Joe. He popped the hood and stormed from the cab, in hopes of solving the problem.

"Didn't you say you were gonna take it to a mechanic and get it fixed?" complained Harvey, rolling his eyes back and sighing.

Billy Joe's guilty smile answered Harvey's question.

Harvey stepped outside in a vain and pointless attempt to assist Billy Joe. He knew absolutely nothing about car repairs. His only contribution was to wear a sad face and whine.

Billy Joe knew about as much as Harvey, concerning car repair. His idea of dealing with the vapor lock meant staring at the engine block in a depressed and oddly comical manner. Seconds passed. Billy Joe turned the key, then cussed wildly in a warm breeze.

Harvey could spew obscenities as well as Billy Joe. The only one who didn't cuss was Corky. His one response to this crisis meant snarling at Harvey. It got them nowhere. After several failed attempts to rev the engine, the trio had no choice but to spend the night at Bishop Springs. The GMC remained a dead horse, and Billy Joe gave up on it.

As a rule, the vehicle would cool enough after long hours of idleness, to eventually fire up and get on the road.

Bishop Springs was the last place Harvey wanted to spend the night. It was hot as blazes out there, even in the shade (and there was little shade). Yet, darkness slowly sat in once the sun had dropped below canyon walls. Soon, it was night. At least Bishop Springs had a toilet. At any rate, there was no point in grumbling. Harvey and Billy Joe resigned themselves to crashing there until morning. To make the situation more bearable, they sat up two lawn chairs and sleeping bags in the back of the GMC. Once bedtime arrived, they'd sleep under the stars. A cool breeze now swept through the canyon.

Harvey slipped on a Grangeford High hoody and reluctantly accepted his fate. He broke into an Igloo cooler, where hotdogs and cold beer awaited him.

Billy Joe fetched his guitar to perform a bit of improv. He created tunes which quickly popped into his mind, and constantly made snide, self-deprecating comments. He'd usually begin by saying, "Now's a song I just know will suit the drunks and lowlife scumbags in Burnside!" or "Here's one I made up outa shits and chuckles!" He'd then break into lyrics involving Spam, marijuana, or Terminal Gravity. The beer caused him to slur his words, and he grew increasingly more vulgar in parodies of well-known country tunes.

Corky and the two boys relaxed, ate granola bars, potato chips and wieners, and sipped beer. The night sky was clear. For the exception of cars zipping along the highway, it remained tranquil and quiet. Anytime someone stopped at the rest area, Billy Joe never mentioned engine problems. Instead, he claimed to be merely "camping out" at Bishop Springs. To Harvey's chagrin, he'd introduce himself as Cheyenne.

No matter how hard he tried, Harvey couldn't get his mind off of Nick Fredericks. He was unable to shake images of Nick walking away, to a frightening and uncertain future. Did anyone else fret over Nick's welfare? Would others offer him a warm bed or a decent meal? Or was Nick completely on his own?

"Billy Joe?" Harvey mumbled, brushing away a mosquito who landed upon his bare thigh.

"What's up?" asked Billy Joe.

Harvey took a deep breath. "What?... What do you think my folks will do if they? ... You know ... if they find out about us?"

Billy Joe snickered. "You mean about us being two awesome, good-looking fellas?"

Harvey rolled his eyes back and sighed. "I mean ... what if they find out about?... ya know ..." Harvey ran his fingers through Billy Joe's hair. "About us?"

Billy Joe giggled. He kissed Harvey on his forehead, then squarely on the lips. "Your folks? 'Mr. and Ms. Pot-Smoking, Twig-Eating, War-Protesting, Voting-Straight-Democrat Madden'?"

Harvey let out a deep breath in frustration. "Whatever ..."

"You honestly think they're gonna get all bent out of shape over us?" Billy Joe swigged down his beer. "Hell, no! First thing they'll do is run to their bedroom and screw, in celebration of raising a gay kid! Next thing they'll do is invite all their liberal friends over to smoke a blunt in ..."

"Billy Joe!"

"You think they'll give a goddamn-go-to-hell about you dating a handsome fella like me?" Billy Joe snickered. "It'll make 'em pleased as punch to know their token gay child is in love with a Mick-Spic-Injun kid! Your mom'll get on the phone to tell all her buddies about us, while your old man'll haul our asses up to the Portland Pride Parade! They'll die happy knowing they got a twinkle-toed fairy in the clan!"

Harvey slugged Billy Joe's arm as hard as he could. It only made Billy Joe laugh even louder.

"Billy Joe!" Harvey screamed. "Or should I call you 'Cheyenne'? You phony-assed, wanna-be-cowboy!"

"What're you getting so riled up about?" giggled Billy Joe, rubbing his aching shoulder.

Harvey's voice revealed panic and fear. "What? What if they freak out and start screaming like they blew it by having me, and?... What? What if they throw me out of the house, and ...? And what if I end up like Nick?"

"You really think that? Drink up, Harve! Christ, they'll love you that much more, if for no other reason than to figure they're raising a gay kid who loves a good-for-nothin', Tater-Eatin', Taco-Bending Redskin. If you ain't black or Jap or the grandson of an illegal spic, like me, your folks'll still brag to their Commie pals 'cause you like guys!" Billy Joe leaned forward to sing in Harvey's ear. "'Beautiful dreamer, wake unto me. Starlight and dewdrops are waiting for thee. Sounds of the rude world, heard in the day, Lull'd by the moonlight, have all passed away'!"

"I'm serious!" shouted Harvey. "I dunno what my folks will do, when ... If ..." He looked straight into Billy Joe's eyes. "I'm scared!"

"What the hell for? Your folks are cool. Cool as all hell! Not as cool as me ..." Billy Joe ran one finger over his mustache. "Trust me, they'll be cool with it, no matter what."

"But what if you join the Army?"

"Well, not over that. But no worries. They'll really be cool when we make it big in Nashville. Me as a singer and you as a writer. And if they ain't cool with us, I always will be." Billy Joe kissed Harvey's cheek, as Corky snarled. "I love you, Harve. Now and forever."

Harvey sat quietly, wondering what his fate would eventually bring.

Near the hour of eleven that night, Harvey and Billy Joe folded the lawn chairs, laid out the sleeping bags, and got ready for bed.

Harvey peeled off this shoes and socks, placed them next to the Igloo, then crawled into a Coleman sleeping bag. He took in a deep breath, and rested his head upon a feather pillow. There, he looked up at the sky toward the Big Dipper. In the distance, crickets chirped as an endless cycle of water rushed through the swift, narrow currents of the Powder River.

Billy Joe also got into his own bedding, next to Harvey. Corky positioned himself between the two boys, acting as a barrier between his beloved master and one he viewed as an opponent.

"I know this ain't exactly Fish Lake," apologized Billy Joe. "But if the rig flies right, I'll have us up there before noon tomorrow."

"I'm okay," answered Harvey. "As long as I'm with you."

Harvey and Billy Joe snuggled and gave each other a warm embrace. Harvey closed his eyes and did his best to quill any worries or doubts concerning his devotion to Billy Joe.

Before dozing off, the last thing Harvey heard was Billy Joe's soft and melodic voice, singing in his ear while occasionally kissing him upon the face and forehead.

"'Beautiful dreamer, wake unto me, Starlight and dewdrops are waiting for thee. Sounds of the rude world, heard in the day, Lull'd by the moonlight, have all passed away' ..."

6

Harvey was awakened by the sudden, loud roar of the GMC's engine, along with the shaking of his bed. He tiredly opened his eyes to see a pale, blue sky above. He blinked a number of times, wondering where he was and how he got there. He looked around to see rugged, canyon walls. He sat up and quickly took notice of the nearby outhouse.

"Got the rig going, Harve," a familiar voice stated. "Get up, we gotta move."

Harvey wiggled out of his bedding, then fetched his socks and shoes. He stretched his legs and back and yawned. Tiredly, he hopped into the cab, where Billy Joe and an angry dog awaited him.

"Morning," greeted Billy Joe, admiring himself in the rearview mirror. Already, he had the car stereo blaring up on high. This time, it was a greatest hits album of Hank Thompson.

Corky warned Harvey to keep his distance.

Bright, fiery streaks of light in a sunrise crept over the hills to the east. A pleasant, cool breeze swept into the cab.

"Good morning," yawned Harvey. "What time is it?"

"About six," told Billy Joe, putting the GMC in gear. The pickup slowly rolled out of the rest area. "We'll stop in Halfway for chow, then head on up to Fish Lake."

"Yeah, sure. We'll head on up to Fish Lake, unless your stupid rig won't start again."

"Ha-ha," responded Billy Joe, in annoyance.

The trio entered Eagle Valley, a tranquil location of rolling green hills, farms, and ranches. It was home to Richland, a town of less than two-hundred residents. It was a quiet village, featuring a couple of restaurants and taverns, general stores, and service stations. Hardly anyone was on Main Street, since most businesses had yet to open. Early risers included a young woman and her black lab, out on a jog, and an older man taking a morning stroll. Two boys left town on ten-speeds and made their way to Brownlee Reservoir, fishing poles in hand.

Within a minute or two, the GMC had left Richland, then gradually accelerated to nearly sixty miles an hour. There was one more hill to climb, separating Eagle Valley from Pine Valley and Halfway.

Halfway was yet another small community, with the Wallowa Mountains to the north and west, and a high-mountain desert to the south known as the Sag. It was the Gateway to Hells Canyon, the deepest gorge in North America.

Years before Halfway had gained notoriety when it became the first dot.com city, and unofficially changed its name to Half.com.

Harvey and Billy Joe exited off of the highway, passed the VFW Hall and Baker County Fairgrounds, then entered Halfway. They stopped on Main Street, across from a well-established diner known as Buffalo Bills.

Billy Joe kept both windows of the cab opened a few inches so Corky wouldn't die from the heat. He offered Corky a couple of dog biscuits and promised to bring him table scraps from breakfast. Corky happily accepted the biscuits, while giving Harvey the evil eye for no good reason other than his mere existence.

Harvey and Billy Joe entered Buffalo Bills. The pleasing, familiar and assuring smell of eggs, bacon, sausage, toast, coffee and hash browns greeted them. The café walls were decorated with a number of elk and deer antlers, along with reproductions of western paintings from Frederick Remington and Charlie Russell. In one corner, a small number of older gentlemen argued politics and religion at a section of the diner known as 'The Table of Wisdom'.

Harvey and Billy Joe took a table next to a window which gave them a great view of the west wall, a mountain range separating the valley from the rest of the world.

A young woman, just out of high school, dashed to the boys' table. She carried silverware, glasses of water, and menus. With a friendly smile, she asked if Harvey and Billy Joe wanted coffee.

Billy Joe answered yes, while Harvey requested orange juice.

Not far from their table, near the center of the dining room, were two teenage girls. Both were dressed in Northern Oregon University sweatshirts, short-shorts, and leather sandals. One had long, straight, dishwater blonde hair, hanging below her shoulders. She had well-tanned, slender yet sinewy legs. The other was considerably shorter, with dark hair rolled in a bun, and round, black eyeglasses which gave her an owlish appearance. Her legs were a ghastly, pale white. The girls reminded Harvey of Daphne and Velma, the female leads in 'Scooby Doo'.

The two girls turned their attention to Harvey and Billy Joe. Both smiled and welcomed them with, "Good morning."

"Morning," responded Billy Joe, kindly tipping his Stetson.

"On your way to Snake River?" the shorter girl asked, in anticipation.

"Naw," answered Harvey. "Fish Lake. Might do some sight-seeking, hiking maybe. Nothing special, really."

"We came in from Elgin last night," the taller girl said. "We're taking a few kids from our church down to go fishing and swimming at Brownlee and Oxbow."

"What church is that?" asked Harvey.

"'Independent Church of Christ'," the shorter girl said. "Non-denom."

"Cool," commented Harvey, lacking sincerity.

"We ain't really here to help kids," the taller girl explained. "That was our excuse to get out of town. We're letting everyone else in our group do the helping. We came to look at guys, raise hell, get drunk, stoned ..." The taller girl stared at Billy Joe. "And laid."

Billy Joe snickered, as Harvey and the shorter girl blushed.

"We might just change our minds about Snake River," the taller girl flirted. "And make our way to Fish Lake, instead."

Harvey and Billy Joe traded glances. Spending time with the two girls might be one thing. Having a few cold ones with them, well, that was yet another story. Neither Harvey nor Billy Joe wished to smoke weed.

And, as far as getting laid was concerned ... Harvey and Billy Joe had plans for that, all right, though it didn't involve the two girls.

"Awesome," said Billy Joe, lacking enthusiasm.

The two girls invited themselves to Harvey and Billy Joe's table. The taller girl introduced herself as Dani, while the shorter one was Debra. They were cousins, and upcoming seniors at Elgin High School.

"I'm Harvey Madden, and this is my ... Best friend ... Billy Joe McBain.

From Grangeford."

"Just call me 'Cheyenne'," said Billy Joe, cleverly rubbing his mustache.

Dani and Debra smirked.

"What's so funny?" asked Harvey.

"We know this ugly fat girl named 'Cheyenne'," explained Dani.

Billy Joe's face altered to a deep, violet blush. Harvey responded with uproarious laughter.

"Reckon I oughta get myself another Old West nickname," mumbled Billy Joe, painfully.

"'Laramie'!" shouted Debra, eagerly.

"'Montana'," suggested Dani.

"'Nebraska'," laughed Debra.

"I got a kid sister named 'Phoenix'," added Dani.

"At least you don't have one named 'Walla-Walla'!" giggled Debra.

"I got one!" offered Harvey. "'Halfway'!"

"That ain't no help," Billy Joe told Harvey, in betrayal and resentment.

"'Milton-Freewater' sounds pretty good to me," kidded Debra. "Then we can call you 'Milty' ... 'Hiya, Milty!'"

"'Laredo'," said Harvey, hoping to get back on Billy Joe's good graces.

"'Laredo'," mouthed Billy Joe, taking time to mull that one out. "'Laredo'. Yeah, I like that, yeah ... 'Laredo'! Thanks, Harve! 'Laredo'."

"So why do you go by the name, 'Billy Joe'?" questioned Dani. "Ain't you too old for that? Why not just 'Bill' or 'William'?"

"Ain't no 'Bill' or 'William' to it. Billy Joe's the name. My full name, on the birth certificate. 'Billy Joe McBain'."

"Whatever." Dani shrugged. "'Billy Joe'. 'Laredo'. 'Slim'. 'Little Black Sambo'."

Harvey glared at Dani in shock and disapproval.

"Well, now that we know who we are and what our names are," said Debra, "can we have breakfast?"

The four teens relaxed to hot coffee, refreshing fruit juices, scrambled eggs, hash brown potatoes, toast, and small talk. Billy Joe and Dani chatted about firearms and hunting. Billy Joe was a life member of the National Rifle Association, while Dani was vice president of a local youth gun club. Both bragged about the various birds and game animals they had tagged throughout the years. Billy Joe was especially proud of a four-point buck he had shot in the wilderness. Most of Dani's trophies involved antelopes in southeastern Oregon. Neither had bagged any black bears yet, though it was on their bucket lists.

Harvey and Debra discussed the arts … music, films, television, literature. Both had a desire to go into creative writing and journalism. Harvey liked classical music, black and white photography and cinematography, science fiction, fantasy, and horror. Debra was into romance books and movies. She liked human interest stories and uplifting biographies.

Debra sat next to Harvey at the table. During their talk she often placed her hand on his shoulder or (more often than not) upon his bare thigh, just above the knee. Occasionally, she complimented and toyed with his long, blonde hair. Her kind smile telegraphed that she wanted more from Harvey than just camaraderie and friendship.

Harvey turned toward Billy Joe, anxiously. He hoped for assurances that nothing "unplanned" would happen with the two girls. Harvey wasn't at all attracted to Debra. She wasn't homely, but hardly a dish. At the same time, the way that Billy Joe conducted himself toward Dani gave Harvey reasons to shutter.

Increasingly, Harvey felt uncomfortable in Debra and Dani's company. He wanted to leave the diner and reach his destination of Fish Lake, where he'd have Billy Joe to himself.

Harvey quickly took notice to Dani's seemingly endless comments concerning Billy Joe's hair, his Stetson, and his mustache. Where Harvey grew embarrassed by Debra's actions, Billy Joe played along with Dani. He often added a bit of self-deprecating and sarcasm to the proceedings. It was enough to make Harvey jealous.

Though Harvey didn't want to say so, the touch of Debra's fingers running lightly along his knee and lower thigh did give him a bit of a rush.

Billy Joe had dated chicks in the past and, despite his relationship to Harvey, regarded himself as bisexual. As a result, Harvey began to wonder if he was on the verge of losing Billy Joe.

However, it was Billy Joe's account of a hunt near the Imnaha River which brought an unexpected end to breakfast. While scouting for signs of deer in a thicket, Billy Joe had to answer a call of nature and found a suitable spot under a pine tree.

Billy Joe grinned mischievously as he explained how he had just dropped his drawers to take care of business, when opportunity unexpectedly came his way. "So, here I am, taking a good old-fashioned country dump, when this humongous five-point stepped out of the brush, about twenty yards away," he said. "Even though this wasn't the time and the place to get off a shot, I couldn't let a chance like this just slip away. Being real quiet, I fetched my .06, took careful aim, and ka-bloom! Sent a round in the buck's direction."

"Then what?" questioned Dani.

"Missed the son of a bitch by a mile," laughed Billy Joe, spitting coffee across the table. "But that wasn't the worst of it! The .06's recoil made me lose my balance and splat! I fell, ass-first, into a huge pile of my own ..."

Debra dropped her fork into a plate of hash browns and gravy, then groaned like she might puke.

"What a fine and pleasant adventure to share over food," said Harvey, sarcastically. "Smooth move, Billy Joe. Real smooth."

"Got it all over my shirt!" cackled Billy Joe. "My vest ... Huntin' jacket ... into my pants!"

"It's about time we were on our way," Debra mumbled. She pushed the hash browns away and got to her feet. "That's a very charming story. Forgive me if I don't share it with our church group."

This was a relief to Harvey. It meant that Debra and Dani would go their separate ways, and allow Harvey and Billy Joe to go theirs. Still, there was agreement that the two girls might again meet with Harvey and Billy Joe, later on.

As the four teens stepped outside, into the bright morning sun, Dani turned to Harvey and Billy Joe and said, "Wanna hear a good one?"

"Sure," agreed Billy Joe, in anticipation.

"What would you call the 'Flintstones' if they were black?" asked Dani.

Harvey and Billy Joe glanced at each other and shrugged.

Dani answered, "Niggers!"

Billy Joe answered with loud, riotous laughter. Not Harvey, who found no humor in the riddle. Instead, he wanted to send Dani flying into the middle of next week. He was torn between letting the offense go, or answering with contempt and rage.

Billy Joe recognized Harvey's anger. "Reckon we oughta mosey on up to the hills," he said, tipping his hat. "Be seeing you lovely ladies. Keep on the sunny side!"

With that, Billy Joe led Harvey to the pickup.

Debra and Dani bid the two boys farewell, and wandered toward a yellow Volkswagen.

As promised, Billy Joe had boxed up some table scraps for Corky. The ornery dog snarfed the treat down, nestled himself tightly against Billy Joe upon the seat, and warned Harvey to keep his distance.

Once the GMC got on the road, Harvey commented on 'Velma and Daphne's' horny behavior toward them.

Billy Joe dismissed Harvey's concerns with a snicker.

"I dunno," mumbled Harvey, his thoughts clouded by fear. "The way Daphne acted around you, I began to think you was gonna pounce on her and ..."

"Me?" questioned Billy Joe. "Why, I reckoned Velma had a'ready jumped you in her own mind."

"I'd never cheat on you, Billy Joe! Though I sometimes think you'd cheat on me!"

"Aw, like hell I will!" shouted Billy Joe, admiring himself in the rear-view mirror. "What makes you say that?"

"Well, just look at the way Daphne ..." Harvey took a deep breath and sighed. "Dani ... The way Dani acted around you."

"Okay. So, whadda you gotta say about Debra sweet-talking you, Harvey-Boy?"

Harvey shifted uncomfortably on the seat, as Corky growled. "Well, for what it's worth," he spoke, painfully. "I despise that loud-mouthed, racist bitch."

"How come?" smirked Billy Joe.

"She seemed too ..." Harvey searched for the right words. "Too arrogant and assured of herself. Like she was the Queen Skank of Elgin!"

Billy Joe laughed. "'Dani, Queen Skank of Elgin and her noble squire, Little Debra Four-Eyes'."

"Not only that," continued Harvey, "I just couldn't stand hearing Dani using the N-word'!"

"Aw, c'mon, Harve. We are from eastern Oregon ..."

"That doesn't matter! People on this side of the state ought to know better than to use racial slurs! You of all people should know that!"

"You're right, Harve," agreed Billy Joe, in guilty delight. "I just know it gives a knee-jerk, bleeding-heart liberal like you tremendous satisfaction being in love with a Mick-Spic-Injun like me."

7

Once Harvey got over being angry at Billy Joe, the rest of the trip went well. It was only twenty-three miles from Halfway to Fish Lake. But the road was slow, narrow, and treacherous. Once the GMC left a blacktop highway, the road evolved into a single-lane, dirt-and-gravel path.

Billy Joe had made this trip many times before. He knew from experience that it was a pleasant trek, which brought sight-seers through an extremely beautiful and breathtaking region. Still, if one wasn't careful, it led to death or disaster for those too cocky, arrogant, or stupid to pay attention to hairpin corners, steep cliffs and hillsides, and slick edges.

The landscape was exciting and gorgeous. It was also harsh, rough, tough, brutal, and unyielding. This was no place for speeding, showing off, or hot-rodding. Rarely did Billy Joe drive above twenty-five or thirty miles an hour. The easier pace gave Harvey time to soak in the high altitudes, evergreen trees, tall grass and other foliage. Squirrels, deer, and even a black bear sprinted across the road.

Billy Joe never accepted the cutesy-pie, sweet, innocent, "Disney-esque" view of Mother Nature. Life was difficult, unpredictable, unfair, and brief for creatures who lived in these mountains. Billy Joe figured that even the tiniest of creatures had more courage and survival skills than braggarts who viewed themselves as 'Rambo'-types.

Harvey concentrated on the scenery around him. Too often, his mind was elsewhere. He loved Billy Joe dearly. He also questioned and doubted the future. Harvey realized that, once Billy Joe entered adult life, he planned to join the military and leave Grangeford. There were always chances that Billy Joe would fall in love with another, and forget about Harvey. Harvey had never loved anyone as much as Billy Joe, and couldn't handle thoughts of a life without him.

Without Billy Joe, who'd I love now?

And who'd possibly love me?

Along the way, the GMC passed an area which had been ravaged by wildfire in 1994. The Twin Lakes Fire had destroyed several thousand acres of forests before it was finally extinguished. Harvey and Billy Joe examined the damage, still evident after many years. Although new-growth trees and foliage slowly took charge, burnt snags and bald ridges revealed the extent and devastation of the blaze.

Neither teen spoke of what they had encountered. In Billy Joe's mind, wildfires were a regrettable fact of life in the western United States and to be expected. Harvey regarded the catastrophe as a sign of mankind's lack of care and consideration of the natural world.

Fish Lake sat at an altitude of about sixty-seven-hundred feet above sea level. An earthen dam was constructed in the early Twentieth Century, to increase storage capacity for irrigation. Fish Lake was stocked with rainbow and brook trout. The Forest Service had built campsites to park and set-up RVs or tents. Outdoor toilets and a boat ramp were available on the lake's north shore. The lake was surrounded by mountain peaks and towering Lodge Pole Pines.

Harvey and Billy Joe found a spot to build their camp, not far from restroom facilities. A Marty Robbins CD played on a portable sound system, as the boys unloaded their gear then erected a canvas tent large enough to stand, dress, and sleep in. They kept Corky on a leash to keep him from causing trouble. The dog growled and snarled at other visitors who greeted Harvey and Billy Joe. The boys engaged in small talk and marveled at the world around them. The scenery, the smell, and the satisfaction of reaching the lake were their rewards. The air was cool and thin, as a cool breeze swept through an untamed landscape.

Although he had two or three changes of clothes, Harvey brought only cut-offs, swim trunks, and khaki shorts to protect his legs from the elements.

Once the tent was put up, Harvey, Billy Joe and an angry dog went inside to enjoy needed privacy. As a celebration, the two boys hugged and kissed as Corky protested out of jealousy. To keep him quiet, Billy Joe gave

Corky some of the tuna sandwiches which Grandma Abigail had made.

Eventually, the teens got into tee-shirts, cut-offs, and beat-up sneakers. Billy Joe replaced his Stetson with a baseball cap and a pair of sunglasses, which he believed complimented his mustache. Later, the trio wandered along the shoreline.

"Despite what ya saw ... Or what you thought ya saw at Buffalo Bills," said Billy Joe, "I'd never cheat on you ... ever ..."

"I hope not!" shouted Harvey, a hint of doubt in his voice.

"I been thinking about this on our way up here. I going into the Army next year. What if, once I finish basic, we get married? That way, you can come with me wherever I get stationed, then ..."

"What if you don't join the Army at all?" argued Harvey.

Billy Joe sighed. "I know you don't understand, but try. Look, just try. I wanna serve our country, defend it, and uphold what I believe is my duty ..."

"What happens if you go to war? What if you get sent somewhere dangerous, and get hurt or ...? Or ..."

"Get killed?"

Harvey turned away from Billy Joe and nodded, 'yes'. "Or what if some of your Army buddies refuse to accept us ... or me? What if they make fun of us, or worse? What if we get treated like dirt?"

"'Oh, I'm a good ol' rebel,'" sang Billy Joe, with a silly grin. "'Now, that's just what I am' ..."

Harvey shook his head in disgust. "Here I am, trying to be serious, and all you want to do is make jokes. Sometimes Billy Joe, I swear ..."

"I love ya, Harve, more than you'll ever know."

"You say that now."

"I say it, forever. I'll keep saying it, until we're both dead. Then I'll say it when we're in Heaven, Hell, Limbo, Portland or Poughkeepsie."

Harvey sighed. His emotions nearly got the better of him. For a moment he wanted to give Billy Joe a tight squeeze, and kiss him on the lips. But there were already a fair number of others at the lake that morning, and Harvey didn't want to make a spectacle of himself. Still, he was unable to hold his feelings back.

For a minute or two, no words were traded. Instead, Harvey and Billy Joe stared quietly across the lake. The surrounding mountains were well above the timberline, and remained covered with thin layers of snow. Fish Lake was only accessible by car for about five or six months of the year.

In the winter, it wasn't unusual for the lake to get twenty feet or more of snow. Still, snowmobilers and winter hikers ventured up there when the lake was covered with deep ice. Avalanches were not uncommon. Only the knowledgeable, strong-willed, well-prepared or foolhardy spent time at Fish Lake in winter. There were those who'd create shelters out of snow, which created effective insulation.

Billy Joe was an outdoorsman. He always dreamed of hiking from Joseph to Halfway through the wilderness, a distance of about forty miles. Billy Joe had chatted with those who made it about a day or two. Countless people had conquered the trek alone. Billy Joe hoped to do it with an experienced guide, and take plenty of time, perhaps two or three days. He wanted to fish the high-mountain lakes and streams, and even swim in fresh, clean water which remained cool and pristine year around. He yearned to sleep under stars, unhindered by city lights, clouds, or fog. He sought to stand upon peaks so high, one could see far into distances of a hundred miles or more. Despite plans of leaving his home state, Billy Joe aimed to remain one born and raised in a state which he loved and cherished dearly.

One can take the boy out of Oregon ...

One can never take Oregon out of the boy ...

8

The morning's silence was pierced by the arrival of an older model Chevy pickup, used to haul firewood. The rig had a good number of miles on it, and proved it in the scores of dents, bent fenders, cracked windows, misshaped and crushed sides. Dust, dirt, and mud decorated the vehicle's exterior. Billy Joe guessed the Chevy dated back to the late Seventies or early Eighties.

The Chevy's back held a couple of chainsaws, along with axes, splitting malls, and wedges. Well-worn and balding tires had somehow sustained the extreme weight of holding a cord or more of wood. The roar of the Chevy's engine spoke of the tremendous effort the vehicle had served its owner throughout the years. The rig resembled automobiles in post-apocalyptic adventures such as 'Mad Max' or 'The Road Warrior'.

The driver was a man in his seventies, who had faced a variety of personal traumas and demons and came out on the other side ... Scarred and shattered and scattered, yet still a survivor. He wore a weathered, tan straw hat over unruly, salt-and-pepper hair. He had long, gray sideburns and stubble upon his lips and chin. His face and forehead were wrinkled and creased. His eyes revealed struggle and sacrifices, along with an unbearable sadness. His features were as harsh as the nearby terrain. His clothes were caked with sawdust and sweat, and hadn't been changed in days. A cigarette dangled from one side of his mouth. The smell of hard liquor spilled from his lips. His teeth were yellow, blackened, and decayed.

The old man stopped the Chevy and greeted Harvey and Billy Joe. The

                    Doug McKim

boys smiled and returned the gesture.

"You fellas interested in he'ping me cut a load 'r two o' firewood?" the old man inquired. This wasn't a casual request, but rather a plea. "Make it right f'r ya. Got my word on it."

Billy Joe glanced at Harvey, his expressions urging a 'yes'.

Harvey was conflicted. He wanted Billy Joe all to himself, yet still felt an obligation to assist the old man. With luck, it wouldn't be an arduous chore. "Sure," agreed Harvey.

"A'right," the old man chuckled. "By God, git in."

The two boys and Corky hopped into the truck's passenger side. Corky sat on Billy Joe's lap and gave the old man and Harvey a snarl. Curiously, he sniffed the dusty, smoke-filled odor within the truck.

The cab was cluttered and littered with cigarette cartons and butts, along with a few tools used to repair chainsaws and other machinery. A gun rack with a .22 rifle and a twelve-gauge shotgun rested at the back window. A bottle of Old Forester sat on the floor, next to the gear shifter.

Harvey looked but found no seat belts to buckle himself in.

"Whatcha lookin' f'r, pard?" the old man asked, switching from second to third gear.

"Seat belts," told Harvey.

"Ain't got 'em," the old man snickered. "Don't use 'em, don't like 'em, don't b'lieve in 'em. Ain't never used 'em since I drove up t' Seattle f'r a buddy's foon'rel, more'n ten years back."

Harvey frowned nervously as Billy Joe laughed and happily went along for the ride.

"Name's Cliff Walker," the old man introduced, flipping a cigarette outside while lighting another one.

"Harvey Madden," the first teen introduced.

"Billy Joe McBain," the other boy spoke, with a clever, self-assured grin. "Just call me Chey ..." He cleared his throat. "Call me ... Laredo."

"Sure it ain't 'Abilene'?" questioned Cliff, clearly unimpressed.

Harvey snickered.

"Fellas from?" asked Cliff, keeping his eyes on the winding road ahead.

"Grangeford," answered Harvey.

"Whatcha doin' over here?" asked Cliff, turning up the volume on a cassette player in the dash board. Hank Snow belted out the song 'Miller's Cave' on an old, warped cassette tape.

"Camping," said Billy Joe. "We work at Big W. I'm a cart pusher, and

Harve's a cashier."

"Like it?" asked Cliff.

"Sometimes," said Billy Joe. "Pays the bills. After I graduate next spring, I aim to join the Army."

Harvey grunted, disapprovingly.

"Got drafted soon as I turned eighteen," said Cliff. "Went into the Marines. Spent time in San Diego, Twenty-Nine Palms, La Jeune, a year 'r so over'n Okinawa. Got me outa Oregon f'r a spell."

"You hear that?" chided Billy Joe, nudging Harvey's shoulder. "Get me out of Oregon for a while. Maybe the both of us."

"Soon as I left the service," recalled Cliff, "I raised me some hell. Drunk ever' night. Chased a helluva lotta nooky. Purty soon the money run out, and I had t' git me a job. Worked in a fillin' station for a spell. Then I joined the Labors Union and worked construction."

Harvey and Billy Joe said nothing. Both found interest in Cliff's life story.

"Started with the tail end of buildin' Hells Canyon Dam on the Snake," Cliff went on. "Went from that t' buildin' the Mason Dam over by Sumpter. Then I he'ped build 'No Name City'." He chuckled. "Ever hear of it?"

Harvey and Billy Joe shook their heads, 'no'.

"Ain't there no more," said Cliff. "Took a helluva lotta money buildin' it just so we could tear it down a few months later. Built for the movie 'Paint Your Wagon'."

"When was that?" asked Billy Joe, curiously.

"'68, I reckon," said Cliff. "Shot most of it by Eagle Creek, not too far from Richland."

"They made a movie around here?" asked Harvey, in disbelief.

"Never saw 'Paint Your Wagon'?" asked Cliff.

"I never even heard of it!" admitted Harvey.

"Aw, just as well I reckon," grunted Cliff. "Long time ago. Don't matter no more. It was a musical, but truth be told no one in it could hardly sing a lick."

Harvey and Billy Joe glanced at each other and shrugged.

"Then I he'ped build the freeway from Ontario clear up t' Portland," said Cliff. "Good money on that job. Damn good money! Then I he'ped put new generators on Oxbow an' Brownlee Dams."

"Sounds like you did real good," said Billy Joe, in admiration.

"Aw, not too bad," agreed Cliff. "Only thing was, I was a'ways away from home. By then I was hitched an' had me a couple o' kids. Family needed me close by. Opened me a bike shop on Tenth Street out in Baker, an' stayed with it clear t' retirement."

"How many kids you got?" asked Billy Joe.

"Five," said Cliff. "One's a lawyer over in Eugene. 'Nother's a pipe liner. Works all over the world, makes damn good money. Daughter's a school teacher up in Yakima. 'Nother daughter got herse'f killed in a car wreck, few years back." Cliff stopped, and somehow kept his emotions in check. "Youngest kid never 'mounted to a damn. Never has 'mounted to a damn. Reckon he never will."

"I have an older brother like that," said Harvey.

"Aw, well hell. Still love 'em," said Cliff, sadly. "Ain't sure I like the worthless bastard. But I'll a'ways love 'em."

"You wanna have kids?" asked Billy Joe, slapping Harvey on the knee. "Don'tcha?"

"Only if they don't break my heart," answered Harvey.

"Hah!" laughed Cliff. "Good luck with that!"

"What do you mean?" asked Billy Joe.

"Sooner 'r later they'll up an' break yer heart," mumbled Cliff. "Come home drunk 'r stoned outa their heads. Whenever you hear 'bout 'em harassin' the neighbors with dumbass pranks, phone calls dealin' with Prince Albert in a can, 'r nigger knockin' on peoples' doors in the middle o' the night. Or when they d'cide t' stand up to yer authority by lookin' at'cha straight in the eye an' tellin' ya to go screw yerse'f."

Billy Joe let out with annoying laughter. Harvey found no humor in it at all. Initially, he winced at the use of the 'N-word'. However, Cliff's comments dug far deeper than that.

Harvey loved and respected Terry and Elaine. He didn't always agree with or understand them. He had yet to upset them. Never once did he bring them shame or embarrassment. In Terry and Elaine's mind, Harvey was the good child, the good son, their pride and joy ...

... Their "little Harvey boy"!

So, what if Harvey pulled something which devastated his parents? Was it a requirement in eventually breaking away from his folks, an attempt at becoming a grown-up when being a grown-up is a necessity? Terry and Elaine loved Harvey, dearly. In time, Harvey had to live his own life, make his own decisions, paddle his own canoe.

Terry and Elaine had reservations about letting Harvey go. But this too was inevitable ... wasn't it? After all, Terry and Elaine were in their sixties and couldn't live forever.

What would be that event which was the first step for Harvey to declare his independence? Would it involve painful and unforgiving words? Would it be a revelation concerning Harvey's relationship with Billy Joe? Billy Joe wasn't just Harvey's best friend. He was Harvey's boyfriend.

The one Harvey hoped to spend the rest of his life with, in holy matrimony ...

And how would Terry and Elaine react to that?

9

Cliff Walker stopped the Chevy in a wide spot on the road, to avoid obstructing traffic. He pointed up the hill just above the road, which was populated with Lodge Pole Pine. "Cut down a illegal tree th'other day," he said, grinning wickedly. "Better haul it off 'fore some Forest Service son of a bitch catches me."

Billy Joe laughed as Harvey rolled his eyes back, sighed, and wondered what he had gotten himself into.

Cliff fetched a Stihl chainsaw from the back, and asked the boys to follow him to a fallen tree he'd cut into firewood. Billy Joe grabbed a splitting mall and two wedges. He had cut firewood with his grandpa, and was fairly competent and capable in it.

The Maddens relied on electric heat, provided in part by solar panels on their roof. For Harvey, thoughts of people heating with firewood seemed outdated, antiquated, and primitive.

And now he was helping cut an illegal tree ...

What have I gotten myself into?

Cliff, Harvey, and Billy Joe wandered to a long, narrow lodge pole that rested upon the ground, about twenty yards above the road. The air was cool and pleasant, as a slight breeze swept through the trees. Cliff sat down on a stump, to check the gas and oil in the chainsaw. "Feelin' a little dry," he said. "Ain't right t' cut wood without a snort 'r two. One o' you fellas get my bottle. Take me a sip 'r two, an' git all fired up. Go right ahead an' take a snort, yerse'ves."

Harvey took a deep breath and released it in a sigh. Reluctantly, he returned to the Chevy for the bottle of Old Forester.

What have I gotten myself into?

Cliff straight-shot from the bottle, then handed it to Billy Joe who did the same. Billy Joe gave the bottle to Harvey, who was partial to beer but disliked hard liquor. No matter. In order to go along and get along, he took a sip.

Cliff found a twig on the ground, and broke it to the length of about a foot. He gave Harvey a pencil and twig and asked him to make marks on the fallen tree, to indicate where to cut. He urged the boys to wear gloves for the job, and stated there were pairs of Green Apes in the Chevy's jockey box.

Harvey picked a mismatched pair of gloves, then used the twig to measure lengths on the fallen tree. Cliff started the saw and divided the log into foot-long blocks. Billy Joe split the blocks into quarters. Brazenly, he showed off his strength and abilities with the axe or splitting mall. He slammed the tools into the wood with a dull, echoing thud! Later, he tossed slabs of firewood into the narrow roadway, next to the Chevy.

Harvey placed the firewood into the back of the Chevy. Occasionally, he crawled in and stacked the wood in what he hoped was a proper fashion. He wasn't in the best of physical condition, and soon grew tired. Cars often passed by. Their passengers happily gave Harvey a wave, even if they didn't know him.

The roar of the chainsaw was deafening and, in Harvey's mind, an offense to his ears and peace of mind. It contrasted with and shattered the peace and serenity of the forest. If Harvey was disturbed by the sounds of the chainsaw, then so were those who called this area home. He now regarded himself as a willing participant in violating the natural world around him, and felt ashamed for it. He wanted to be a guest in these hills, and not someone stealing from them.

And yet, if Harvey had no right in cutting firewood, then what right did he have sitting up a tent at Fish Lake?

It didn't take long for the log to be removed, and the Chevy fully loaded with firewood. The three men were covered with sawdust and sweat. Harvey kept his negative views to himself. He wasn't able to get a word in edgewise, considering Billy Joe's boasting and bragging of his woodsplitting skills. Cliff had tagged the load of firewood, and wanted to take some time to rest in the shade of a thick growth of trees. The trio traded the bottle of whiskey, and feasted on stale pork rinds.

Harvey had never cut firewood before, and was conflicted by it. While he tried gaining a sense of satisfaction in helping Cliff, he could've lived without the knowledge of harvesting an illegal tree. He also resented the sawdust caked on his face, hair, clothing, arms and bare legs.

"You taking this load to your place?" inquired Billy Joe.

"Ain't f'r me," answered Cliff. "Sellin' it t' someone not too far outa town. Two-hundred-an-fifty dollars a cord. Don't burn it myself. Can't. I live in a thirty-foot travel trailer in Pine Creek." Cliff pronounced 'creek' as 'crick'.

"You and your wife?" asked Harvey.

Cliff shook his head, 'no'. "Wife ain't with me no more. Died some years back."

Harvey and Billy Joe gasped.

Cliff's eyes revealed sadness and despair, though his voice upheld composure and control. "Lost damn near ever'thing tryna save 'er. Damn doctor bills took ever'thing. Lost the place in town tryna keep 'er alive. Lost damn near ever'thing, an' in the end I lost 'er."

"Sorry to hear it," whispered Harvey.

Cliff wore a smile even though he clearly suffered tremendous pain. "Sorry as hell f'r a lotta things. Sorry she ain't here tell me t' dress nice, an' shave ever'day. Sorry she ain't here t' fix my meals, an' keep house an' keep me from bein' a slob. Sorry she ain't here t' fall asleep with, an' wake up next to."

Harvey and Billy Joe faced each other, yet said nothing. Meanwhile, Corky took an interest in a squirrel next to the Chevy, though Billy Joe refused him a chance to pursue it.

"More'n anything I'm sorry she ain't here t' tell me she loved me, and f'r me t' say I love 'er," said Cliff, taking a swig to ease his nerves. "Don't just cut wood t' make an extra buck 'r two in my old age. Cut wood to gimme a reason t' git up in the mornin', and keep me from goin' off my head 'cause she ain't here. Cut wood t' keep me from missin' 'er so god-damn bad."

Harvey looked at the ground next to his feet, feeling worse as Cliff went on. He wondered if life would treat him so unfairly, assuming he lost Billy Joe in such a way.

"Whoever you fellas fall in love with an' marry," Cliff spoke, his voice barely audible. "Spend ever' minute ya can with 'em, 'cause ya never know when they'll up an' leave ya, an' never come back."

Moved by what Cliff had just said, Harvey was compelled to give Billy Joe an embrace and shower him with kisses. This wasn't the time or place for displays of passion. Even then, Harvey was overcome with emotions. Fears of losing Billy Joe, be it through words of anger, falling out of love, or death, were unspeakable. Harvey wished to spend every waking moment with Billy Joe. If Billy Joe was to die first, then Harvey would gladly follow him into the Hereafter that very moment.

Harvey found it impossible to openly reveal his love for Billy Joe, be it in acts of affection and tenderness, or even in speech. Instead, he slowly reached out, placed one hand upon Billy Joe's shoulder, and gave it a gentle squeeze.

Billy Joe responded by looking Harvey squarely in the eyes. A warm smile, along with a teardrop or two seeping from one eye, said more than words dared to utter.

10

Billy Joe and Corky went with Cliff to deliver a load of firewood to a customer. Meanwhile, Harvey returned to the tent to relax. He was covered from head-to-toe in sweat and sawdust, and wanted only to be clean again.

For the moment, Harvey also wished to get away from Corky, away from Billy Joe, and away from the needs and expectations of others. He loved Billy Joe, yet got fed up with his bragging and showing off. Billy Joe was very capable with axes, wedges, and malls. Yet, his arrogance infuriated Harvey.

Harvey entered the tent and collapsed upon a sleeping bag. He slowly removed his filthy clothes, and gave himself time to contemplate in the nude. The tent's interior was hot, stuffy, humid, and claustrophobic. But Harvey needed this moment to sort out his own thoughts and worries.

Harvey couldn't stop fretting over Nick, and wondered how the homeless teen was coping. He couldn't imagine what it was like to spend the night in a park, sleeping on a bench, wondering about your next meal or if you'd be victimized. What did it mean to survive long, cold nights? Was there a church, a family, or social service agency willing to help Nick, and secure him a safe future? Harvey struggled to realize that Nick wasn't his responsibility. In the end, Nick had to be responsible for himself.

So, why did Harvey feel a need and burden to rescue Nick? And would anyone come to his rescue, should he find himself in similar circumstances?

Harvey also pondered Cliff's words, once the trio finished cutting wood. Cliff was a guy in his seventies, stubble on his face, with a noxious smell of tobacco smoke and whiskey on his breath. Surely, he had been young once. All elderly people were young before they grew old! From stories and photographs, Harvey had proof that Terry and Elaine were young, years ago. In a way, Terry and Elaine acted much younger than many people in their sixties. Terry remained physically active, maintained strong hope and optimism, and had a never-say-die attitude.

Terry and Elaine didn't seem particularly old. And, yet, eventually they'd age.

Eventually, they'd die.

No one wants to think of their own deaths, let alone the deaths of loved ones! Yet, everyone must face mortality, don't they?

Including Harvey and Billy Joe!

Harvey imagined himself at age thirty. He then visualized himself in middle age, when his hair took on a salt-and-pepper appearance ... When creases and wrinkles scarred the face, eyes, and forehead. Muscles sagged, waistlines expanded, dreams faded and died. Aging was a truth that all had to work through ...

Including Harvey and Billy Joe!

Not only did Harvey love Billy Joe. He was in love with him! Would their love remain, not only in youth, but clear to old age?

Billy Joe was a handsome guy, even with that idiotic mustache. Would he forever remain attractive? Would Harvey still be drawn to him, in years to come? Would he remain faithful and devoted? Was Billy Joe the love of a lifetime? Or were the two destined and doomed to break up? If so, would Harvey find another to love, and be in love with?

The world outside grew louder and livelier, to the point where it destroyed Harvey's silence and solitude. Several vehicles roared back and forth. Tourists strolled through the campground. There was the frustrating growl and buzz of a boat speeding across the lake. Harvey wished to stay secluded, lost in his own thoughts while struggling to make sense of his own life and existence.

Harvey sat up and glanced outside, to a sunny and inviting afternoon. Like it or not, he had to get dressed, take a dip in the lake, and have fun!

Harvey slipped on a pair of shorts he planned to use as swim trunks. Modesty nearly prevented him from wearing them. Harvey usually wore shorts, providing they didn't show too much skin. He had a nice tan on his knees and shins. But his thighs had gained little sun, and were a ghastly pale.

Harvey spotted a teen girl wandering by, wearing a violet, long-sleeved tee-shirt and short-shorts. Her legs were far whiter than Harvey's! Therefore, if this young lady wasn't bashful in her lack of a tan, then why should Harvey be ashamed of his own appearance?

Harvey got into his shorter-than-usual-shorts, a worn-out, white tee-shirt, and leather sandals. He took a deep breath and, mustering his courage, left the tent. Self-consciously, he wandered to a nearby wooden-planked dock.

The comforting sunlight, gentle breeze, and spectacular scenery granted Harvey calm and tranquility. His took a moment to surrender his shyness, then ventured onward.

Harvey went to the end of the dock. He sat at the lake's edge, removed his sandals, and dipped his smelly feet into the water. The lake's temperature felt icy, compared to the heat of the day. At first, Harvey gave up any ideas of swimming. Still, he was filthy from cutting wood, and wished to clean up prior to Billy Joe's return.

Harvey counted to ten, held his breath, closed his eyes, and bravely took the plunge.

After the initial shock of submerging himself into the murky depths, Harvey held a peaceful celebration where he rejoiced in being young and free. Nothing else mattered ... Not the well-being of Nick Fredericks, not his relationship with Billy Joe, not his job at Big W, or whether his parents knew he loved another guy. It was enough to simply allow his troubles to wash away.

Moments later, Harvey crawled back upon the deck, shivering, with his teeth chattering. He had forgotten a towel to dry himself on.

Harvey sat quietly for several minutes, when two boys sprinted onto the deck. He guessed their ages at twelve or thirteen. Neither were especially tall. Both were scrawny and thin. The two boys were dressed in flip-flop sandals and skimpy, black swim trunks. One was a lad with brown hair, cut neatly above the neck and ears. He had bright, green eyes, and an enthusiastic smile.

What Harvey immediately noticed was the boy's skin tone which clearly lacked character or color. Indeed, the boy had the palest hide that Harvey ever laid eyes on! For the exception of his face and arms, the boy had no sign of a tan anywhere. This was easily noticeable on the legs and torso, which were so white that Harvey found them nearly unsightly and grotesque.

And yet, the boy didn't seem to care. He was more interested in having a fun-filled afternoon at the lake.

The other boy was Asian, perhaps of Japanese descent. The Asian was taller than his buddy. His had long, black hair which dangled below his shoulders. His face was long, thin, and narrow. He was practically skin and bones.

Harvey found many Asian males to be gorgeous, and this kid was no exception. His first crush in the sixth grade at West Grangeford Elementary was a Chinese kid who, unfortunately, loathed and despised homosexuals.

The two boys greeted Harvey, and hoped their presence didn't disturb him.

"Naw," responded Harvey, smiling. "Make yourselves at home."

The two boys sat upon the deck, debating on who'd be the first to jump in.

"It takes some getting used to," told Harvey. "But once you hop in, you're gonna love it."

"Wanna join us?" the Asian boy invited.

Harvey shrugged and, without a second thought, leaped back into the lake. "Go for it, fellas!" he shouted. "The water's fine!"

The two boys began wrestling on the deck, attempting to throw the other into the water. Laughing, they grappled until both went in at the same time, locking arms and legs. After an explosive splash, the two boys finally emerged from the depths, giggling and kidding around.

Eventually, Harvey and the two boys returned to the deck, soaked. They sat together, gradually drying off and shivering from the icy water.

"I'm Harvey. Harvey Madden," the older teen introduced himself. "From Grangeford. I'm here with my ... my friend Billy Joe. Came to spend a few days up in the mountains."

"Rodger Derry," the Caucasian boy said, shaking Harvey's hand. "This is my brother Ken."

"Your brother?" questioned Harvey.

"My soon-to-be brother," said Rodger, proudly.

"Okay," said Harvey, seeking illumination.

"His dad's marrying my mom," explained Ken, excited at prospects of having Rodger as a sibling.

Harvey smiled. "Cool. When's the big day?"

"In a few weeks," said Rodger, placing an arm around Ken's shoulder.

Harvey couldn't help but to be touched at the apparent love shared by Rodger and Ken. Already, the duo acted and almost looked like brothers. Chances were, they even fought, bickered, and made up like brothers. Harvey envied Rodger and Ken, along with the bond they'd hopefully develop in the future.

You had lunch yet?" Rodger asked Harvey.

Harvey shook his head, 'no'.

"Why don'tcha join us?" invited Ken. "We got hamburgers, hot dogs, potato salad, soda pop."

"No, thank you," Harvey politely refused. "My ... friend should be returning shortly, and I ..."

"Aw, c'mon!" insisted Rodger. "We won't bite. I promise!"

Harvey took a deep breath and sighed. "Sure, why not?" he agreed, reluctantly. "Guess I can drop by for a few minutes. Lemme run back to my tent, and dress in something more ... appropriate."

Harvey rushed to the tent. There, he got into a pair of gray shorts and a red, long-sleeved, Grangeford High tee-shirt. He felt conflicted and awkward about invading the two boys' camp, invited or not. Who was he to sit down and break bread with complete strangers? Who was he to impose upon those outside of friends and family?

11

Harvey stepped from the tent, where Rodger and Ken awaited him. "Thanks for the invite," he said, a slight blush on his face. "I can't stay too long, though."

"How come?" asked Ken.

"My friend should be back any moment," told Harvey, unable to conceal his anxiety.

Rodger and Ken led Harvey to their campsite about fifty yards away. Harvey followed them with a tired, self-deprecating grin. The two younger boys entered the camp like they owned it. Next to a couple of large tents was an older model, silver Dodge Caravan, with an extended wheelchair ramp.

Harvey remained standoffish, knowing he was a guest and wishing to behave as such.

"Well, good afternoon," greeted an attractive, Asian woman in her mid-to-late thirties. She kept her hair in a ponytail, and wore round, steel-framed eyeglasses. She was dressed in a blue plaid-shirt, sleeves rolled to the elbows, cut-off jeans, and sandals. She stood about Harvey's height, thin and apparently athletic and physically fit. "My name's Angela Tanaka," she introduced herself, shaking Harvey's hand.

"Harvey Madden," he said, tugging at his collar. "I ... I'm from Grangeford. Just here for a few days, me and a ... buddy, who should be back any moment."

"Go ahead, have a seat," ordered Angela, directing Harvey to a lawn chair.

Harvey sighed. "I don't mean to impose ..."

"You're not imposing," stated Angela. "We saw you sitting alone on the dock. I told Rodger and Ken to go get you. Thought you might like some company."

"Thanks," snickered Harvey.

"I noticed how polite you were to my two sons while you guys swam together," said Angela, stepping toward a grill where burgers, fries, and hot dogs sizzled over coals. "Don't worry, Harvey. If I thought you were a creep, I would've told you to get lost before you even set foot in our camp. Now, how do you like your burger and hot dog?"

"Well done," said Harvey, gradually permitting himself to relax.

Angela offered Harvey a glass of iced tea and prepared a paper plate of food.

Quietly, Harvey observed his hosts. Aside from Rodger, Ken, and Angela, there was a small girl of about eight. Harvey guessed the girl was Ken's biological sister. She was tiny in stature, wearing a bright blue tank top, shorts, and sneakers. Next was a boy of Rodger's size and age. He wore a silver sweatshirt, baggy, plaid shorts, white socks, and a black stocking cap. Long, dark hair concealed his ears and eyes. He sat silently in one corner, listened to music through earphones, and paid Harvey no mind. His facial features and skin tone resembled Rodger's.

Finally, there was a woman of around seventy in an electric wheelchair. She also wore a tank top and shorts. Harvey thought the older woman's clothing was inappropriate, considering a severe weight problem which made her appear bulbous, even grotesque. The older woman's belly threatened to work itself out of the tank top. Her legs were nothing but globs of fat, unappealing to look at.

The small girl was Angela's daughter, Candi. The boy with the stocking cap and headphones was Rodger's twin brother, Rodney. The woman in the wheelchair was Barb, Rodger and Rodney's paternal grandma.

"So, whadda you do at Big W?" Barb asked Harvey.

"I'm a cashier," answered Harvey, shifting uncomfortably on the lawn chair.

"How long've you been there?" asked Barb.

"Close to a year now," snickered Harvey.

"Full time?"

"Uh ... no." Harvey wondered if this would lead to a game of 'Twenty

Questions'. "Well, during school I only do weekends and some holidays."

"What about now?" asked Barb, retrieving a cigarette from a pack she purchased from a store at the Umatilla Reservation.

"Thirty-five hours a week." Harvey sipped his iced tea.

"How come just thirty-five hours?" asked Barb, inquisitively.

"Store policy. Since I'm ... ya know ... Still a minor."

"How old are you, Harry?"

"'Harvey'!" corrected Angela, realizing that Barb's constant questions troubled her guest. "And I'm guessing his age is ..." She took a moment or two. "Seventeen?"

Harvey laughed. "Close. Sixteen. I'm sixteen."

"Heavens!" gasped Barb. "You didn't drive up here alone, did you? On that sorry excuse of a road?"

"I ... I didn't drive up here, at all ..."

"Then how'd you get here?" pressed Barb.

"I came up here with my ... my best friend ... Billy Joe McBain."

"And where's he?"

"Oh, Barb!" snapped Angela, sitting a dish on a folding table next to Harvey. "Please stop being so nosey, and give him a chance to eat his lunch!"

"I'm an old woman," responded Barb, "and that gives me a right to be nosey."

Harvey looked at the meal which Angela gave him. There was a thick hamburger decorated with lettuce, slices of tomatoes and onions, and smothered in relish. Egg salad, carrot and celery sticks, and a small bag of Lays potato chips completed the feast. Harvey fetched a plastic knife sitting next to the dish, cut the burger in half, and took a bite. Obsessively, he upheld good table manners.

"You like your job at Big W?" Barb went on.

Harvey shrugged in a way to suggest, 'so-so'. "It's a job."

"Thinking about staying there after you're done with high school?"

Harvey laughed, and nearly choked on the food. The situation wasn't so much funny, as it seemed bizarre and unbelievable! He couldn't understand why Barb insisted on knowing practically everything about him. At the same time, he wouldn't be rude.

Harvey shook his head, 'no'. "Soon as I'm out of high school, I plan to go to college." He swallowed a mouthful of food, then sipped the iced tea. "Maybe Northern Oregon, Oregon State, or the U of O ..."

"What for?" asked Barb.

Harvey shot Barb a glance, as it to ask what for what?

"She wants to know what you plan to study," explained Angela, sitting at a lawn chair next to Harvey.

"Um ... Creative writing," Harvey mumbled, hoping and praying it wouldn't bring on yet another round of questioning.

"Where's the boy you come up here with?" asked Barb, smothering her cigarette into an ash tray.

"Billy Joe?" asked Harvey. "He went to haul a load of firewood to someone in Halfway."

Barb frowned. "You came over here to cut firewood?"

"Not ... Exactly. I ... we got ... roped into it. Ya see, some old guy came along and ..."

"So, who's this Billy Joe?"

"My ... friend?" Harvey grew increasingly ill-at-ease.

"You think you might want to invite him over, soon as he gets here?" asked Angela, politely.

"Well, I'm not so sure," chuckled Harvey, digging into the salad. "I know he'd be more than happy to have a bite of this really terrific food, but he's got this mean, ugly-assed dog ..." He stopped. "I mean ... an ornery hound dog, and I'm not sure how that'd go over with your kids."

"Doesn't sound to me as if you like your friend's dog," noted Angela.

"I don't," confided Harvey. "I don't like Billy Joe's dog, at all. I don't like him, he doesn't like me, and ..."

Harvey was interrupted when Rodger and Ken got into a wild wrestling contest. Both sought Harvey's attention, while showing off what they perceived were their "considerable" abilities. In the course of just a few seconds, all they managed to do was nearly knock over the tent shared by Angela, Barb, and Candi.

Ken sent Rodger somersaulting in Harvey's direction. Rodger came within scant inches of getting his bare feet into Harvey's plate of food, and caused the glass of iced tea to splash upon the ground.

"Rodger! Kenichi!" scolded Barb, in a shrill voice. "You stop that horsing around, right this instance!"

"But he started it!" claimed Rodger, pointing at Ken.

"And I'm stopping it!" shouted Angela. Hastily, she retrieved the spilled glass of tea sitting near Harvey's feet, then fetched another one. "I'm so sorry!" she apologized. "I hope none of it got on your shoes or socks!"

"Oh, not quite," responded Harvey, in a mixture of shock, frustration, and muted humor. "Close ... But not quite."

Angela filled another glass of iced tea for Harvey, then turned toward Rodger and Ken. "I want you two numbskulls to get out of your swim clothes," she commanded, "and into something more suitable!"

"But, Mom!" protested Rodger.

"No 'but's!" snapped Angela, pointing at the boys' tent. "Go in, get dressed, and come out when you can act more like men!"

Ken and Rodger went to their tents to get in hoody sweatshirts and cut-offs. Harvey felt ashamed. While he wasn't exactly thrilled with their nonsense, he hated seeing the two boys get hollered at. He now wanted to return to his own campsite, away from a painful "family drama". He hoped not to make it look so obvious.

Meanwhile, Rodney sat in one corner, listening to his music while endlessly playing a handheld video game. He seemed totally oblivious to everyone and everything around him.

"Well, you know a little something about me," commented Harvey, sarcastically. "Enough to bore you to tears."

"Harvey!" laughed Angela, giving a gentle slug to her guest's shoulder. "Believe me, you're far from boring!"

"I'm glad someone thinks so," spoke Harvey, biting into his hamburger. "If you don't mind my own curiosity. Rodger and Ken tell me you're about to get married."

"That's right," volunteered Angela. "To Rodney and Roger's father."

Harvey looked all around the campground. "Where's he?"

"My fiancé Kurt?" questioned Angela. "He had to stay home. He works as a contractor in The Dalles, and believe me ... He's got his hands full. Jobs coming in left and right. We'd been planning this trip for weeks. Kurt really wanted to come with us, but he just couldn't. So, Barb and I loaded the kids up in the van and went without him. It's too bad, too. He would've loved it!"

"It is nice up here, isn't it?" Harvey glanced at Barb and smiled. "I'm guessing you must be Kurt's mom."

"I have been, his entire life," chuckled Barb.

"I divorced Ken and Candi's father a few years ago," admitted Angela, "when I found out he was more interested in his secretary than he was in me or the kids."

"I'm sorry," mumbled Harvey.

"Don't be," commented Angela. "It was a long time coming and, believe me, I'm a lot better off."

"And?" Harvey shot a glance at Rodger and Rodney.

Angela leaned forward to whisper in Harvey's ear. "Their mom died about a year ago. Lung cancer."

Harvey nodded his head in affirmation, but said nothing.

"Barb's living with us," Angela went on. "Thought it might be easier on the boys, that way. A lot easier on me, that's for sure. Kids can sure be a handful!"

"I guess," snickered Harvey, chewing on a celery stick.

"Now the whole brood's gotta put up with me," commented Barb, lighting another cigarette. "Whether they like it or not."

"Oh, c'mon!" said Harvey, in a comedic tone. "Surely you can't be that bad!"

"Wait until you get to know me a little better," commented Barb.

"I'll keep it in mind," responded Harvey.

"Bet you got a lovely young lady waiting for you in Grangeford." commented Barb, mischievously. "Is she a blonde, a brunette, or a redhead?"

Harvey nearly choked on egg salad. Insecurity, self-consciousness, and fear took charge. Sensations of overwhelming heat and suffocation nearly overtook him. Harvey began to think he was on the verge of going off his head, dying, or both. A deep-red blush painted his face, as nervous laughter escaped his lips.

The situation wasn't funny as much as it felt unspeakable and horrific. Harvey almost felt insulted and violated by Barb's line of questioning, but who was to blame? He was in love, but not with a blonde, brunette, or redheaded female. He liked guys---- and the guy in question was Billy Joe! Harvey wasn't about to share this to his hosts. And he damned sure wasn't about to admit that he was gay.

Few people were aware of Harvey's sexuality. That's the way he preferred it. His love life wasn't Barb's business! Still, he didn't want to become angry or offended, then end up saying or doing the wrong thing.

Harvey wondered if his silence said more than he was comfortable with. Did his lack of a response essentially voice an awkward truth? And, if he attempted to conceal truth with a lie, would the lie tell on itself through his apparent apprehension?

It wasn't enough to say that Harvey contemplated on fleeing from the campsite. He wanted to disappear completely, and retreat to a safe place where he'd be safe and unthreatened by inquiries involving a private matter.

Seconds passed by like minutes. Harvey's fear and insecurity grew so out of control they nearly got the better of him. He honestly thought they were his undoing. He struggled to find answers for Barb's silly and innocent question, and found no solutions.

Therefore, the best Harvey could do was respond with an impish grin and a shrug.

Angela sensed Harvey's discomfort. "Would you care for another hamburger?" she asked, to change the subject. "If you want, I can give you a re-fill on your iced tea."

Harvey was about to answer with a polite 'no' when a loud, beat-up woodcutting truck neared the campground.

12

Harvey turned to see Cliff Walker's truck stop by his tent. Billy Joe and Corky stepped out of the vehicle. Billy Joe fetched a bright red, ten-speed Huffy bicycle from the back. He glanced through the passenger side window and wished Cliff a nice day.

With that, the truck did a U-turn and roared away.

"Over here!" shouted Harvey, waving eagerly. He sat his paper plate on the folding table, excused himself, then dashed to Billy Joe. "Where'd you get the bike?" he asked.

"This is our payment for helping Cliff," answered Billy Joe, happily. "He gave it to me, and I'm giving it to you."

Harvey's mouth dropped open as he stared at the bicycle. It wasn't necessarily one bike, but rather pieces of several bikes, cobbled and welded together from parts which Cliff kept in a tool shed near his trailer. There was tremendous craftsmanship and care in constructing the bike. The frame had been put together, flawlessly. Nothing clashed or seemed out of place. There were no dangers of the bike falling apart.

Finally, Cliff had painted the frame in a glossy, shiny red, giving it a beauty and sheen.

"This way you can ride to work and back," said Billy Joe, displaying the bike like it was a work of art. "Whadda ya think, Harve?"

Harvey was nearly moved to tears. He felt awkward to accept that which he regarded as a gesture of love and kindness. "So, what did Cliff give you for helping him?" he asked.

"Nothing. Cliff tried to offer me something, but I figure a handshake was good enough. But this is what he gave you."

Harvey threw his arms around Billy Joe. Corky released a snarl in response.

"Well," invited Billy Joe. "Give it a whirl."

Harvey got on the Huffy and rode it along the distance of the drive-through. It was in excellent condition, and glided as if to travel in the air. After taking a couple of laps along the drive-through, Harvey showed it off to Angela, Barb, and the four children.

Rodger, Ken, and Candi examined the bike with awe and curiosity. All wished to take it for a spin. The only youngster seemingly unimpressed was Rodney, who concentrated on his games and music.

"You guys can take it for a short ride," accepted Angela, reluctantly. "But you have to promise to be really careful with it."

Billy Joe placed Corky on a lead and wandered over to see who Harvey chatted with.

"This is my ..." Harvey cleared his throat. "My friend ... my best friend, Billy Joe McBain. We both work at Big W."

"Howdy." Billy Joe tipped his hat. "Name's Billy Joe, but you can call me 'Laredo'."

Rodger, Ken, and Candi gave each other looks of surprise, shock, and slight humor. Angela let out a silly little snicker, as Barb began singing a classic tune. "'As I walked out in the Streets of Laredo,'" she recited, with a wry grin. "'As I walked out, in Laredo one day' ..."

This knocked the wind out of Billy Joe's sails.

"So, what moronic nickname are you gonna go with next?" questioned Harvey, sarcastically. "'Tucson'? 'Salt Lake City'? Kentucky Fried Chicken?"

"At least my folks didn't name me after an invisible, six-foot rabbit," commented Billy Joe. With a pathetic James Stewart impersonation, he added, "Harvey ..."

Harvey shrugged. His mind wasn't on Billy Joe. Rather, he stared at Barb who, despite her appearance, sang rather well. The words of a traditional cowboy ballad came out naturally, like she was born to perform music. Barb's voice had a rustic tone to it, which stemmed from a remote, backwoods, in-the-middle-of-nowhere small town, boasting a single-lane gravel street and one small business which served as restaurant, tavern, market, and drugstore. Barb didn't possess the voice of an angel, but one born in the heartland of America, where everyone knows everyone along with their deepest secrets, and people drive the same car for twenty years or more.

Billy Joe noticed this, as well. He used this opportunity to sing the second verse of 'Streets of Laredo' in a deep baritone.

With that, Billy Joe and Barb gave each other familiar smiles. They were members of a fraternity, joined in common knowledge, understanding, and appreciation. Both belonged to a fellowship of musicians, and were delighted to make a fortunate acquaintance.

Harvey came from a background which favored good health, and an obsession in image and care for a temple known as the human body. Due to Barb's obesity and reliance on an electric wheelchair, he initially categorized her as a fat slob, lacking in nutritional smarts, drive, or self-worth. Likely, the woman ate herself to the deplorable shape she found herself in now, and had no desire in dieting to avoid an early death. Harvey's attitude toward Barb had modified. Instead of viewing a disgusting person, Harvey granted Barb greater sympathy. Perhaps it wasn't her fault that she had evolved into a "walrus', cruising around on mechanical legs. Harvey kept his opinions to himself, yet desired to know more about this woman who shared a love of music with Billy Joe.

Once Billy Joe and Barb finished the duet, Angela and Candi responded with encouragement and applause. Rodger and Ken looked on with astonishment and amazement.

Rodney stayed in his tiny corner, lost in his headphones and oblivious to everything around him.

"Awesome!" complimented Billy Joe, enthusiastically. He sat in a lawn chair next to Barb. "How? ... Where? ..."

"I was a lead singer of a Portland-based band in the 70s and 80s," explained Barb. She beamed proudly as her mind returned to youth, washed away by the cruelty of time, loss, shattered dreams, gray hair and wrinkles. "We played all around the Willamette Valley, clear up to Federal Way. Did a couple of gigs in Vancouver." She snickered. "Vancouver, British Columbia, not Washington. Even did a show or two in San Francisco. Mainly we performed at county fairs, here and there, get-togethers in city parks, and more honky-tonks and filthy dives than you can imagine."

"Okay," mumbled Billy Joe, hoping he had found one to learn from and become inspired by. "What was the name of your band?"

"Oh shit, we had a buncha names!" giggled Barb. "'Warm Springs Reservation'. 'The Portland Trio', 'The Willamette Quartet'. 'The Vagrants of Burnside."

Billy Joe grinned.

"Changed our names whenever members came or left," Barb went on. "We even tried to just call ourselves 'Portland'. You know, back when groups like 'Kansas', 'Boston', and 'Chicago' were the thing. Tried to capitalize on the different kinds of music we played."

"Such as?" asked Harvey.

"Aw, folk, rock, country, rock-a-billy. This was around the time when the 50's tunes got popular again, so we did a lotta the 'doo-wop' stuff. We played whatever people wanted, and the style changed because of whatever kinda audience we played for, or what was big at the time."

Billy Joe shrugged. "So, why'd you stop playing?"

"Oh, for a lotta reasons." Barb sighed. "We all went our own ways. Artistic differences, ego, arguments of who was boss and who was right, the gigs we'd sign up for and what stages we'd play on. We even got some airtime on Oregon Public Broadcasting, and blew that one from bickering, even when the cameras were rolling."

"Damn," whispered Billy Joe.

"We all had bigger concerns," added Barb, in resignation and melancholy. "My son Kurt was born, and he needed me more than the band did. We couldn't seem to keep a drummer the whole time we were together. Drummers came and went. We had more drummers than the number of years we played. One got this girl knocked-up, and had to take responsibility for it. Another fella joined the Air Force, and I ain't seem him since. Another guy moved to LA and tried his luck as a solo act. Don't think anything ever come of it."

"Billy Joe wants to go to Nashville and be a country singer," said Harvey.

Billy Joe answered with a cocky smile.

"Sure hope ya make it," said Barb. "Hope ya go farther with it than I ever did."

"Well, whether you made it or not," Billy Joe said. "Something tells me I might learn from ya. Hate to admit it, but I sure need some advice."

"What do you hope to learn from me?" chuckled Barb. "Other than getting banged up in a horrible car wreck, getting arthritis in your whole body, then growing fat and ugly in this damned wheelchair?"

Both Harvey and Billy Joe laughed, uncomfortably. In particular,

Harvey felt shame for his earlier thoughts on Barb.

"'C'mon, ma'am," urged Billy Joe. "I might end up blowing it myself, but I'm sure gonna try not to. Harvey can tell you how much music means to me, just as much as I can. Please? Anything you can tell me to keep it going and not get ... Well, as you said ... all 'banged up'?"

"Aw, I dunno," said Barb, eyeing a small motorboat as it gracefully skidded across the lake. "Just do what you think is right. Take smart advice, do the kinda music you wanna do, don't let some so-called expert try and tell ya what to play or even how to play it. I never made it to Nashville. Always wanted to go. Ya might not get rich or famous, but ya might just make out a'right, playing in the clubs or as a back-up picker for someone else. I can't really tell you what to do. You gotta figure that one out for yourself."

After a moment or two of silence, Billy Joe asked, "What instruments did you play? Or were you just a singer?"

"Strummed a bit on guitars, banjos, the fiddle."

"Hot damn!" cheered Billy Joe. "I knew you was all right, the moment I first met'cha! Hold on right there. I'm gonna mosey on over to the tent and fetch my guitar and banjo! Hope you're up to some jammin' tonight!"

Barb was excited to show her stuff. She hadn't handled a string instrument in the longest time, and hoped she still "had it".

Angela prepared more burgers and hot dogs on the grill, and asked Billy Joe what he wanted.

"Gimme a burger!" requested Billy Joe. "Burn it! Burn the moo right out of it! Then slap everything on it, with loads of mayo!"

Billy Joe went to his own tent, then returned with a guitar and an old banjo. Angela fixed him a burger, a scoop of egg salad, and a glass of Coke.

Billy Joe sat back down next to Barb, and happily offered her the banjo. Barb took the instrument, examined it for a second or two, then dared to play a tune from her own imagination. Billy Joe enjoyed the meal that Angela offered him, while he tuned his guitar and got ready for some serious strumming. He gladly chowed down a second burger, and shared stories about performing at middle school and high school events in northeastern Oregon. He treasured the value of an audience, but realized he was nowhere near the level of Barb's background. He hoped to spend much of his senior year doing shows. To Harvey's dismay, Billy Joe spoke of his plans to join the Army. Afterwards, he hoped on making his way to Nashville with Harvey.

Rodger, Ken, and Candi wished to befriend Corky. Initially, Corky refused to grant them any affection. Only when Billy Joe ordered Corky to cool it, did the dog allow the kids to first touch, then caress him. After a tense minute or two, Corky finally shared love and kindness in return.

Once the guitar was tuned, Billy Joe rested it on his lap. With a broad smile and a mischievous twinkle in his eye, he said, "This is Harve's favorite ballad."

In a noticeably gravel voice and an annoying Southern accent, Billy Joe sang, "'Oh, I'm a good ol' rebel, Now that's just what I am. For this fair "land of freedom", I do not give a damn! I'm glad I fought against it. I only wish we'd won! And I don't want no pardon, for anything I done!'"

Harvey rolled his eyes back and sighed. He believed that song represented the worst in American history and human nature. The only reason Billy Joe played it was to agitate him. Harvey found no humor in Billy Joe's behavior, and knew he did such things to belittle him. More than anything, he wanted Billy Joe to stop. No matter. Billy Joe laughingly shared the song with his hosts.

It further upset Harvey when Barb joined Billy Joe in the second verse. "'I hate the Constitution, This great republic too. I hate the Freedman's Bureau, In uniform of blue. I hate the nasty eagle, With all its brag and fuss. Them lyin', thievin' Yankees! I hate 'em ...'"

"Can we play something more modern?" interrupted Harvey, making no attempt to conceal his disgust.

"Why don't you play a song where the kids can join in?" suggested Angela. She left the grill to sit next to Harvey. She threw one arm around his shoulder, seeking to quell his anger and frustration.

"'Oh, I wish I was in the land of cotton'!" responded Billy Joe, fighting back an urge to laugh. "'Good times there, are not forgotten! Look away! Look away! Look away! Dixieland!"

Barb then began to perform The Battle Hymn of the Republic. Both struggled to drown out the other.

Harvey and Angela gave each other a glance and, as if to read minds, let out with The Battle Cry of Freedom. Both practically shrieked out the lyrics, "'The Union, forever! Hurrah boys, hurrah!'"

Rodger, Ken, and Candi glared at the older members of the party, who sang louder and louder as if they were in a competition. None of the youngsters understood or appreciated the relevance in this nonsense.

Corky eventually won the day by growling, barking, and howling in shrill protest.

Meanwhile, Rodney remained in his own little world, goofing around on a cell phone, oblivious to it all.

13

Throughout the afternoon, Billy Joe and Barb entertained and often led the others in well-known folk, gospel, and Celtic tunes. This gave the campsite a laid-back and pleasant feel to it. From time to time, Barb gave Billy Joe pointers on the guitar and banjo, then demonstrated them by singing traditional verses and hymns.

Billy Joe watched, listened, and learned. Barb was honest about her own mistakes, shortcomings, and failings. She described how crowds and audiences differed, whether she played in small-town taverns or classy night clubs, to civic organizations or churches, fundraisers or sunny Tuesday afternoons in a park. She was honest in her own limitations. She explained which sorts of promoters to avoid, and the importance of remaining persistent and humble. Everything was a lesson, and failure remained a better teacher than good fortune, success, or luck.

Billy Joe took it all in, even as teen confidence and bravado struggled to believe that he was immune to the potholes and blunders in the lives of artists. Barb remained encouraging, but rarely held back in speaking words of warning and caution. She wished Billy Joe the very best, yet reminded him that nothing worthwhile came easy, or without costs.

The others either listened to the tunes which Billy Joe and Barb sang together, or engaged in conversations between themselves. Rodger and Ken made a few more trips to the dock to swim in the cool, refreshing waters of Fish Lake. Angela insisted they allow her or Harvey to act as lifeguard.

Harvey gladly accompanied the two boys during their swims. He remained on the dock, uninterested in getting wet. In the distance, he heard Billy Joe and Barb belt out lively and spiritual duets on Amazing Grace, In the Pines, and House of the Rising Sun.

Harvey increasingly grew envious of their musical abilities, and suffered feelings of worthlessness and inferiority. He feared his own talents as a writer couldn't hold a candle to Barb or Billy Joe's drive and enthusiasm.

People love live music. One doesn't have to do anything but casually sit back and listen. Great musicians bring a smile to the face. Folks may have their own tastes and styles when it comes to singers and songwriters. But love of music is universal. It ties audiences closer together.

Writing is another matter. It's usually a solitary activity, executed in the confines of a study, a bedroom, or the secluded corner of a public library. Even if writers spend long hours in taverns or diners, hunched over a table with pen and paper on hand, they remain lonely and alone. Writers can be surrounded by a hundred people or more, and still experience the pleasures or dread of isolation. Writing often stems from experiences and memories of pain, when authors recollect and recall moments where they've been hurt by the mean-spirited and thoughtless words and actions of others. Even a prosperous day of writing causes tremendous exhaustion.

Reading a good story or book also requires effort on the part of others ... And seemingly fewer and fewer folks have a desire to place time or effort in reading! There are those in society who, once it's no longer required of them, will never take the time to read novels, short stories, or even online and physical magazines and journals.

Musicians are outgoing and extroverted. They prefer the company of others and are empowered by onlookers. Writers can be reclusive and introverted. They often find solace in their own company, yet feel threatened or endangered when in large groups.

It isn't fair! In the end, everyone loved guys like Billy Joe McBain, who not only wanted to be the center of attention but in truth the Center of the Universe! Meanwhile, Harvey Madden feared he was destined and doomed to reside and eventually perish in the cruel darkness of obscurity. It was never a question of Harvey being forgotten. No one would even remember him! Lovers of music may continue to listen to a collection of Billy Joe McBain songs, even after he is dead and gone. Meanwhile, one would have to search long and hard in dank, dusty corridors to even find anything written by Harvey Madden!

And it sucked ...

It really sucked ...

***

Nightfall approached, where marshmallows and hotdogs were roasted over an open flame. There was the telling of comical tales or spooky ghost stories. Rodger and Ken traded their swim trunks for faded cut-offs and hoodies. Everyone got around the warm, inviting fire, sipped iced tea, lemonade and soda, and enjoyed various treats.

Even Corky got into the festivities. He befriended Rodger, Ken, and Candi, who sneaked him hot dogs and s'mores.

A breeze swept over the mountains and lake, as countless stars decorated the skies above. Billy Joe and Barb performed one song after the next. The others gathered around to treasure the moment. Rodger and Ken told riddles and jokes, and Candi became a chum to Corky. Even then, the dog refused to take Harvey out of his sight, and reminded him never to get near Billy Joe. Rodney stayed within his own little world, away from family. Harvey and Angela fed the flames with dried wood and used paper dishes and cups. They made sure the youngsters had enough to eat, while reminding them to finish their plates. Everyone assumed their roles, and assured fun and excitement in this gathering.

Around the time of nine-thirty, Angela asked Harvey to follow her into the tent she shared with Barb and Candi.

Harvey entered the tent, where Angela awaited on a sleeping bag laid out upon the ground. She placed an electric, Coleman lantern between her and Harvey.

Harvey plopped himself on a pillow in one corner and crossed his legs.

Angela looked deeply into Harvey's eyes. "You may think it's a secret," she spoke, quietly, "but something tells me it never has been."

Harvey's heart skipped a beat. Fear jolted through his body like a lightning bolt. He snickered inadvertently, as a blush covered his face. He posted on an impish grin and shrugged.

Angela motioned outside. "How long have you and Billy Joe been ... A couple?"

Harvey attempted to deny Angela's implications. His actions, behavior, and emotions gave him away. He wanted to run away and hide. The cat was clearly out of the bag! If Angela harbored suspicions concerning Harvey and Billy Joe, then who else did the same?

"It's nothing to be ashamed of!" cried Angela, apologetically. "I don't want to put you on the spot!"

Harvey's throat tightened, as beads of sweat rolled from his forehead. Anxiety and panic revealed themselves in his eyes. He felt helpless and trapped. The walls of the tent seemingly closed in, giving him inescapable sensations of claustrophobia. He searched for any defense mechanisms in order to defuse the situation.

"It's nothing to be ashamed of!" repeated Angela. "Love is love, and if you two love each other that much ..."

"But this is eastern Oregon!" shouted Harvey. "Some people might see it differently!"

"Some people think The Dalles is eastern Oregon. Of course, in this state, anywhere east of Troutdale is eastern Oregon."

Harvey and Angela smirked.

"I know it makes no sense," said Angela. "But we live in a world where some people can't stand the sight of a thirty-something, Japanese broad marrying a middle-aged white guy. Some people can never approve of that. Some people will never approve of it. Just like some people can't accept gay writers, or even gay cowboy singers. But you know what, Harvey? I don't care what some people say! Love is love. I love Kurt and I adore his two sons, as if they were my own. The kids get along ... mostly, in a weird, little 'Brady Bunch' sort of way. Oh, sure. They fight over what belongs to who, but it's slowly getting worked out."

"I hate Billy Joe's asshole dog and that stupid mustache," admitted Harvey.

"That dog worries me. He hasn't snapped at the kids, yet. He seems like he could at any moment." Angela smiled. "As far as that mustache ... I'm sure Billy Joe looks better without it."

"Billy Joe doesn't think so. He thinks it makes him look cool, like Tom Selleck or Burt Reynolds ... or somebody."

"What do your parents think about you two?"

"They ... they don't know," stuttered Harvey, fidgeting as he bit a fingernail. "Mom and Dad know we're very close ... Billy Joe and me. But I don't think they know ... Y' know ... that we're in ..." Harvey tied two fingers together.

"They don't know?"

Harvey shook his head, 'no'.

"So, what is it?" asked Angela. "Are you like … afraid they're gonna kick you out, or what?"

"'Or what'," mumbled Harvey, uncomfortably.

"What are your parents like?"

Harvey sighed. "Old hippies. Pot smokers. Anti-war. Anti-everything Republican. Unconventional as hell. Cool in some ways. They stick out like sore thumbs in Grangeford."

"Why do you think they'll be upset with you?" asked Angela, in doubt.

"I dunno," whispered Harvey. "I'm just afraid they'll freak out. It might cause a big stink, even if they show me the door or not. It'll become a huge drama and home won't seem like home anymore."

Angela patted Harvey's knee. "Well, I might be wrong, but I'm sure you'll be okay."

"I sure hope so," voiced Harvey, doubtfully.

"My brother Kerry is gay," confided Angela. "And yeah, it created a rift when he came out. Most of my family's fine with it. There's a few who'll never talk to him, and they'll flat refuse to even discuss it."

Harvey's eyes widened.

"Some people don't get my relationship with Kurt," chuckled Angela. "A white Republican guy and a liberal Japanese broad. But I love Kurt. I try to look beyond politics, or race, or skin color. I'm sure my grandfather in Hiroshima wouldn't know how to handle it, if he was still alive. My own parents are concerned about how Ken and Candi might be treated by Kurt's extended family. Aunts, uncles, cousins and such. I know some people will never support you and Billy Joe. But if you love someone enough, like I love Kurt and his sons, why must I hold back in jumping the broomstick?"

Harvey began to relax in Angela's company. Still, did her opinion bring him any closer to coming out, or coming clean, to Terry and Elaine?

Or to anyone else?

"Well anyway, Harvey," added Angela. "Love is love. If you love Billy Joe enough, and if your parents love you as much as I suspect they do, things will work out. Who cares about skin color or race or politics or sexual orientation, when it comes to the one you wish to spend the rest of your life with? Love is love. And if no one raises a fuss, or selfishly stands in its way, then love will always be love, and love always wins out in the end."

Harvey and Angela heard Billy Joe and Barb happily strumming away, outside. With her raspy yet still breathtaking voice, Barb sang the Sixteenth Century English ballad, Barbara Allen.

"I love that song!" cheered Angela.

Harvey smiled in agreement, then took a deep breath.

"Let's dance!" giggled Angela.

Harvey gasped. "What?"

"Let's dance by the campfire!" Angela hopped to her feet and practically dragged Harvey outside.

Harvey smiled nervously and shook his head in refusal. No good. Angela was undeterred in her desires to swing a hip, and forced Harvey to join in.

Harvey reluctantly followed Angela, where everyone snacked on hotdogs and marshmallows while listening to the music. No one expected seeing Angela throw her arms around Harvey. With her body pressed tightly against his, she moved to the soft, sad tune.

The youngsters turned their attention toward Harvey and Angela, who did a slow dance by the fire. Rodger responded with a giggle, as Ken and Candi wondered if their mom had dropped Kurt in favor of Harvey. Billy Joe answered with a shrill rebel yell, while Barb made the most of this magical moment in the Wallowa Mountains.

Harvey threw his arms around Angela's waist. Little by little, he got over any level of shyness or humility, and simply went along with it.

Though he never admitted it, Harvey couldn't help but to notice how tender and sweet Angela felt in his arms. No question about it, she possessed a beautiful spirit. Harvey felt oddly envious of Kurt, whoever he might be. Angela was quite special, and remained kind and understanding toward him. Harvey experienced a tremendous sense of gratitude to Angela, and questioned if he'd ever repay her for what she told him earlier.

Well, perhaps this dance was a means of settling a debt. Therefore, Harvey did his best to square it with her.

Corky crawled under Billy Joe's chair and held vigil over his master.

The only one in the campground who remained oblivious to this event was Rodney, who continued studying his cell phone, enjoying his own taste in music, and remaining within the confines of his own thoughts.

14

Minutes before the hour of eleven at night, it was time for bed. Angela directed the youngsters to their sleeping quarters. Meanwhile, Billy Joe turned on the flashlight of his cell phone, then led Harvey and Corky to their own tent.

Despite the cooler temperatures, Billy Joe and Harvey's tent was hot, humid, and musty. Although it compromised privacy, the tent's flaps were kept open to let fresh air in.

It had been a long day, and Harvey needed sleep. To his dismay, the world around him held a harsh, primitive, 'outdoorsy' atmosphere and feel about it. The sounds of water pounding against the shoreline, the breeze slapping against the canvas tent, and the chirping of crickets reminded him that he was now in the mercy of Mother Nature. Still, he treasured the camaraderie and friendship which developed between him and his evening's hosts. He missed the safety and accommodations of his bedroom in Grangeford, with its air conditioning and nearby bathroom. On the other hand, he'd spend the night in the arms of his best friend, closest companion and love of his life, Billy Joe McBain.

Corky was another story. The dog continued to growl, snarl, and snap whenever Harvey showed Billy Joe any affection.

A kerosene lantern illuminated the tent. Harvey slipped off his shoes and socks, then tossed them in one corner. He worked out of his shirt and shorts, and wore only a pair of white briefs. He got into his sleeping bag. Billy Joe also undressed, then crawled into bed next to Harvey. He was worn-out yet happy from the day's activities. Too exhausted to make love, he settled on cuddling with Harvey instead.

Moths and other insects circled the lantern.

Billy Joe and Harvey traded kisses upon the face, forehead, and lips, as Corky responded with threatening growls.

"Corky," warned Billy Joe, shutting down the kerosene lantern. The light faded slowly away. This left only the bright moon shining through the doorway. The sounds from outside grew oddly still and quiet. In the distance, someone played an old Johnny Cash tune on a tinny, portable CD player.

Corky shuffled into the sleeping bag and nestled between Harvey and Billy Joe. There, he exhaled hot, smelly breath from his moistened nose and mouth.

"Billy Joe," whispered Harvey. "Angela's onto us."

"Huh?" yawned Billy Joe.

"Angela's onto us. She knows ... About us."

"What does she know?" questioned Billy Joe, mockingly. "That I'm a rootin'-tootin', super cool, straight-shootin' cowpoke? And you're a jittery nerd who carries on like a scaredy-cat virgin?"

"Billy Joe! Angela knows that we're ... a couple."

"Yeah, a couple of awesome guys!" Billy Joe laughed. "What about when you and Angela cut a rug around the fire? I got to thinking maybe you two were a couple! Go to sleep, Harve."

"But what?... What if the others know, too?"

"What of it? I love you, Harve," said Billy Joe. "Why should I apologize for my feelings about you? You're not apologetic about me, are you?"

"Of course not." Harvey rested his head upon Billy Joe's shoulder. "I love you, too. More than anything."

"Then why should I care what others say or think about us? I want you with me, forever."

"Sometimes ... I'm just ... scared, that's all."

"What of? People?"

"What if it's worse than that?" argued Harvey. "What happens if someone tries to hurt us? I mean, really tries to hurt us? Not with words, but with violence? What if we're ganged up on and ...?"

"We'll fight back, that's what!" stated Billy Joe, firmly. "Might get our asses kicked. They'll know they been in one helluva brawl. I'd lose my life if it meant saving yours. I'll die if it comes to that."

Harvey closed his eyes. "I love you more than anything! Even if you tell everyone to call you 'Pecos Bill', or even 'Calamity Jane'."

Billy Joe sighed.

"I'd love you more if you got rid of that ugly caterpillar on your upper lip." Harvey giggled.

"Fat chance of that, pal. Wish in one hand and shit in the other, see which one fills us the fastest. The mustache stays." Billy Joe scooted next to Harvey and, in a whisper, began to sing Abide with Me.

Harvey squeezed tightly against Billy Joe, and gradually fell asleep.

15

Harvey woke a few minutes after five in the morning. He didn't rest well. The sleeping bag he shared with Billy Joe and Corky became a torture chamber of disturbing dreams, which encouraged and feasted upon thoughts of inferiority and worthlessness.

The countless rocks nailing him in the back didn't help, either.

How on Earth did Angela know of Harvey's relationship with Billy Joe? Was it that obvious? How did she figure it out so quickly? Did Harvey unconsciously telegraph it? And, if Angela knew, who else was aware of it?

What if Harvey's parents already knew or suspected that he was gay, and simply never brought it up?

Harvey crawled out of bed. He was exhausted, but preferred getting up. Better to face the day than lie there and constantly be troubled by fears and uncertainty.

It was a chilly morning, and Harvey couldn't dress quickly enough. He slipped on a Northern Oregon University sweatshirt, a pair of cargo shorts, ankle socks, and sneakers. He stepped outside to clear his head.

Already, there were subtle hints of fall in the air. A cool breeze swept through the mountains, as a thin haze of fog hung over the lake. Glimmers of the sun peeked over the hills and evergreen trees in the east. Clouds appeared to be on fire. Spectacular hues of red, brown, orange, and yellow streaks of light illuminated turquoise skies above.

A small herd of deer wandered through the campground, feeding on grass. Harvey remained still, hoping not to startle them. He quietly folded down a lawn chair and sat down, as the deer passed by. Briefly, a doe and two fawns turned to face him.

The visual splendor was enough to quill any doubts Harvey had about an existence of God. Nature was harsh, brutal, uncompromising, and picked no favorites when it came to survival. There were no assurances that one or more of the deer that Harvey had spied upon would be killed by a predator, later in the day. That was reality, the cold hard facts of life. Still, Harvey couldn't deny the magnificence of what he gazed upon. He considered himself lucky and blessed to have an opportunity to appreciate what he had witnessed before him.

It also made him feel small, puny, insignificant, and inconsequential.

Harvey's time on Earth would be far too short. The lake, the mountains, and the majority of trees existed long before he was born. Chances were, they'd remain long after his death ... Unless mankind's shortsightedness and stupidity destroyed them all.

It God had created the lake, the mountains, and the trees, then did God also create Harvey Madden and Billy Joe McBain?

And was it God's will for Harvey to fall in love with Billy Joe? Did Harvey have any say in the matter? If it was God's plan for Harvey to be gay, then should he be thankful or it? Or was his sexuality an act of nature ... perhaps even a fluke or an accident?

Or was it a cruel joke, played on Harvey by a force of evil?

Sadness and confusion overwhelmed Harvey. Anxiety and panic nearly took control.

Harvey's fears and melancholy stopped when Angela and Ken stepped out of a tent in their campsite and wandered toward him. Both were dressed in long-sleeved tee-shirts, athletic shorts, sneakers, and smiles. They greeted Harvey with a cheerful, "Good morning."

"Good morning," responded Harvey, admiring the Tanakas in their willingness to meet the day in an upbeat manner. He began to let go of his own personal demons, and simply hoped to find solace in their company.

"We thought we'd go on a jog together," announced Angela, rubbing her bare thighs while doing stretching exercises. "Want to join us?"

"I really don't believe in running," snickered Harvey, "unless there's something after me. But if you don't mind slowing it down to a casual stroll, then I'm in!"

Angela and Ken agreed.

Despite the chill of the early morning, Harvey was warmed by the rugged beauty of his surroundings, along with the kindness that Angela and Ken granted him. Although Angela knew of his sexuality, Harvey felt secure with her. Ken may have known as well, but posed no threat. In truth, Ken was happy to have another guy tag along on their jaunt.

Once the trio left the campgrounds and headed toward Twin Lakes, they chatted like equals. No ugly remarks or mean-spirited insults were traded. They simply enjoyed a brisk stroll in the woods. It was enough to savor the rewards of friendship, even when it proved temporary and short-lived. Harvey had never once set eyes on Angela and Ken, prior to the day before. Chances were, they'd never meet again, once the two camps went their separate ways. Still, Harvey prayed he'd remember Angela and Ken for the rest of his life, and cherish them eternally.

It wasn't long before the sun extended above the horizon.

The trio stopped for a short breather near a sign post reading the distance to Duck Lake. They rested in a shaded spot, where the atmosphere was deathly quiet and the air calm and still. Harvey swept away an ant crawling up one leg and, hoping to make pleasant conversation, asked Angela about her past jobs.

"My share of retail, and more," stated Angela, in self-deprecating humor mixed with frustration. She took a sip from a twelve-ounce bottle of water, then handed it to Ken. "Fred Meyer, Safeway, Costco ..." She smiled. "Big W."

Harvey took in a deep breath, rolled his eyes back, and sighed.

"Spent a year or so as an office manager for Bonneville when we lived in Hermiston," Angela went on. "Now I'm doing online studies, planning to get a degree in social work. Even though I'm about to marry a staunch Republican, it won't keep me from my duties as a chairperson for the Wasco County Democrats."

"Wow," snickered Harvey. "You sound just like my parents."

"Kurt's got his views on guns, immigration, and abortion," said Angela. "I'll continue upholding needs to assist undocumented aliens or the homeless, equal pay for minorities, a woman's right to choose." She patted Harvey on the back. "No matter what, I'll never abandon my support for gays and lesbians."

Harvey said nothing. A fiery blush spoke for him. He let out a nervous chuckle, but remained silent.

"Remember what I said about my brother, Kerry?" said Angela, noting Harvey's anxiety. "He was like a father to Ken and Candi before I met Kurt. Kerry lived with us for a while to help out with the bills. He made his lifestyle known to the kids, and trust me ... they're okay with it."

Harvey rolled his eyes back and sighed. He glanced at Angela, managed a labored smile, and simply mouthed thanks. Hoping to change the subject, he asked, "Okay. So, what's the story with Rodney?"

"What about him?" questioned Angela, clearly guarded and defensive.

Harvey suddenly wondered and worried if he had brought up a forbidden and troubling subject. No matter. Angela demanded an answer from him. "I ... please forgive me," Harvey apologized." It's just that ... he's so ... well, he doesn't say much, does he?"

"Rodney misses his mother something terrible," explained Angela, tiredly.

Harvey slouched. "I'm sorry if I offended ..."

"No, no," said Angela. "Rodger and Rodney might be twin brothers, but they're as different as night and day."

"That's an understatement," commented Ken, with a strained smile.

Harvey leaned against the sign post.

"Where Rodger always hung out with Kurt," whispered Angela, "Rodney always favored his mom. Kurt likes being outdoors, doing hard labor, macho guy stuff. Rodney wasn't one to leave the house, or even his mother's side. They were more like best buddies than mother and son. They had a bond which nothing or no one could break." Angela hesitated. "But then, when ... when the boys' mom died, Rodney fell apart. From what Kurt and Barb told me, he couldn't stop crying, or learn to deal with her passing. It got so bad he had to be hospitalized. Thankfully, we got him a prescription of anti-depressants, along with an absolutely marvelous therapist in Hood River." Angela took in a deep breath, and slowly let it out. "Rodney's getting better ... A lot better. Honestly, we didn't think he'd be able to make this trip. He's gone a long way since ... Well, since she died. But he still has a long way to go."

"Sorry," repeated Harvey, shaking his head in humility and embarrassment. "Guess I shouldn't have brought it up."

"No worries, Harvey," laughed Angela. "I know that ... Well, I know that Rodney's a strange kid. He'll snap out of it. I hope. Until then, guess we'll just keep loving him as best as we can, and keep our fingers crossed."

16

After a mile or two, Harvey, Angela, and Ken turned and wandered back to Fish Lake. Harvey was saddened, as a very special moment neared its end. Occasionally, his eyes dampened and voice grew raspy. He didn't wish to let go of the ties he developed with the Tanakas and Derrys. He suffered a painful realization that his relationship with them would soon end. Harvey voiced a desire to stay in touch with that family, be it on social media, letters in the mail, phone calls, text messages, Christmas cards in December and birthday wishes throughout the year. Perhaps it was too much to ask, and Harvey felt heartbroken.

Once they reached the lake, Harvey thanked the Angela and Ken for allowing him to accompany them.

"No prob," laughed Ken.

"I loved every minute of it," said Angela, reaching out to softly rub Harvey's face. "You're a fine young man. I hope that, whatever road you take in life, it leads to endless joys and happiness."

Harvey released a sob. He threw his arms around Angela, then gave Ken a hug as well. "I love you guys," he said.

Angela responded with a giggle, though obviously she was moved by Harvey's sentiments. "We love you too," she said. "Can we expect you and Billy Joe over for dinner, tonight?"

"I'd like that!" accepted Harvey, wiping a few tears from his eyes. "Thanks so much for the invitation. You guys are way awesome!"

"We try," commented Ken, as he and Angela wandered to their own campground. "See you later!"

"I'll be then," answered Harvey, barely audible in the early-morning breeze. He stopped to watch Angela and Ken disappear into one of their tents. Seconds later, he entered his own quarters, where Billy Joe and Corky still slept.

Once Harvey entered the tent, Corky slowly crawled out of the sleeping bag. The dog gave Harvey a menacing look, snarled in warning, then went to one corner where he chewed on a dog biscuit.

Billy Joe rolled from one side to the other, mumbled something under his breath, then fell back to sleep.

Harvey sat in the corner opposite Corky, and reached into the cooler for a beer. It may have been too early in the morning for "a cold one", but he sought to take the edge off and relax. He rested against the cooler, sucked in a couple of deep breaths, and struggled not the think.

Good luck with that ...

After a few sips, Harvey snacked on a granola bar. To his dismay and frustration, Corky took interest in his breakfast. Reluctantly, Harvey tossed Corky a piece of granola, to keep the greedy dog happy.

Moments later, Billy Joe peeked his head out of the sleeping bag to see Harvey sitting alone. "Well, good morning 'Sunshine'," he yawned, sarcastically.

Harvey rolled his eyes back and sighed. By now, he was lost in melancholy and fogginess, brought on by beer.

Billy Joe hopped out of bed, then slipped on a pair of jeans and a short-sleeved, blue-plaid shirt.

Harvey glanced up from his beer., "Whadda ya got going today?"

"You remember them two chicks we met yesterday?" asked Billy Joe, working into his cowboy boots. "Daphne and Velma?"

Harvey nodded, 'yes'. "What about them?"

"Daphne mentioned something about a shooting contest this afternoon," said Billy Joe.

While Terry or Elaine were not hardcore gun control supporters, they didn't want firearms in the house. And while Harvey didn't mind going out to shoot with Billy Joe on occasion, thoughts of spending the afternoon hearing guns go off, along with the hoops, hollers, and cheers which went along with it, were the pits. He preferred spending the day alone with Billy Joe in a small diner, or exploring nature, just the two of them. If the opportunity presented itself, perhaps they'd make love. While Harvey and Billy Joe kissed and cuddled on a regular basis, it had been a while since they had sex. And Harvey wanted it … Really wanted it … from Billy Joe.

"Boozing a'ready, Harve?" commented Billy Joe, reaching for a leather case which held a 12-gauge shotgun. "You okay?"

"I dunno," mumbled Harvey, staring at the fade, gray walls of the tent. He quietly sipped the beer as Corky snarled and snacked on granola.

"Must be in love," snickered Billy Joe. "Who is she? 'Little Debra Four-Eyes'?"

"No," grunted Harvey, in annoyance. "I love a bitch. A real bitch. A downright, cheap-assed whore. Just who the hell do you think I love?" Harvey shook his head. "Sometimes I wonder why."

"I never wonder why." Billy Joe grinned. "I never once wondered why I love you. Why should I? Hell, I won out in the deal."

Harvey said nothing as he fought back his emotions.

"What's wrong?" questioned Billy Joe, in a caring yet firm tone. "Still worked up about that Nick kid, or what?"

"I dunno." Harvey gulped down his drink. "I tend to get worked up about everyone and everything."

"I noticed. Everyone and everything. You get all boo-hoo and sappy about everyone, except yourself."

Harvey resented Billy Joe for what he had just said. Yet, he had a history the need of others above himself. Several people, Elaine among them, believed Harvey constantly neglected his own happiness if it meant helping the less fortunate. Harvey did things to please friends and family, often at his own expense. Seemingly, he cared more for others than for himself …

Which worried those who loved him the most, including Billy Joe.

"Cheer up, Harve," said Billy Joe, as he stepped outside. "Come with me to the shooting match, and wish me luck. Watch me win a few prizes, and make the competition look retarded."

Harvey finished his beer and slowly got to his feet.

Billy Joe smiled and slapped Harvey on the butt. "Let's get going! Don't wanna be late to the doings, where I'll show them folks from Halfway who's boss!"

17

Billy Joe left Corky in the care of the Tanakas and Derrys. Harvey was thrilled not to have Corky along. He only hoped that the dog behaved himself, and didn't eat the children.

Billy Joe placed a Waylon Jennings CD in the stereo, and sang along to 'Amanda' and 'Luckinbach Texas'. Harvey preferred that to Bob Wills. Still, he was more accustomed to 60s and 70s rock in the family kitchen at Grangeford, where Elaine prepared meals or gossiped over the phone. He was also fond of the Bach, Beethoven, Mozart, or Carl Orff booming from a sound system in the study, where Terry smoked weed and argued politics over the phone.

The GMC parked in front of Buffalo Bills, a few minutes after eight in the morning. Harvey and Billy Joe entered the diner. There, they found Debra and Dani sitting at a table which offered a great view of the nearby mountains. The two girls were dressed in tee-shirts, cut-offs, and sandals.

Dani made sure everyone in the restaurant had a good look at her. Without a doubt, she was a "hot chick," and went to great lengths to make herself such. Meanwhile, Debra sat across the table, wearing her owlish glasses, hair in a bum, and ghastly, pale legs which stood out in an offensive manner, at least in Harvey's mind.

"Well, if it isn't the Lone Ranger and Tonto," greeted Dani, sipping herbal tea. She glanced at Harvey and added, "How's she hangin', Ke-mo sah-bee?"

Harvey rolled his eyes back and sighed.

Billy Joe sat next to Dani, as Harvey took his place next to Debra and wished her a good morning.

"Good morning," answered Debra.

Dani looked Billy Joe up one side and down the other. The expressions in her eyes gave Harvey reason to worry. "We were just talking about driving up into the mountains to hunt you down," said Dani. "But, now that you're here, what's the plan today?"

"Getting in on that shooting contest," answered Billy Joe in anticipation. "Me and my 12 gauge are hell-bent on sending a few clay pigeons to the Promised Land."

"You got what it takes to knock me and my Mossberg down a peg or two?" Dani questioned, her eyes perking up.

Billy Joe leaned back as he tipped his Stetson forward. "If you don't mind getting shown up," he said, confidently. "I'll give you a lesson you ain't likely to forget. Aw, sure, you'll wanna forget. You'll wanna forget, real bad. But ya never can, and ya never will."

Dani slapped the palm of her upon the table, which echoed throughout the diner and caught the attention of other patrons. "You're on!" she shouted. "I'm gonna send you back home to Mommy, whimpering and whining like an ass-beat pup!"

The waitress approached the table carrying a tray with glasses of water and silverware. "Breakfast?" she asked, cheerfully. "Sorry. I try to remember names, but I just can't seem to recall ..."

"Dowd," answered Billy Joe, in an especially bad James Stewart impersonation. "Elwood P. Dowd." He reached into the pocket of his plaid shirt and handed the waitress a wrinkled receipt from Big W. "Here, let me give you one of my cards. Two martinis. One for me, and the other for my friend Harvey."

Harvey rolled his eyes back and sighed.

Dani and the waitress stared at Billy Joe in confusion. Only Debra got the joke.

"Don't pay any mind to Billy Joe," said Harvey, maintaining a straight face though his tone expressed sarcasm and apology. "We're not sure if he suffers from psychotic episodes, or if he's just a moron."

Dani and the waitress snickered.

"Smooth move, pal," grunted Billy Joe. "See if you get a blowjob from me tonight."

Dani exploded in riotous laughter, as Debra gasped.

"I ... I'll go get some menus," the waitress stuttered, then hastily returned to the kitchen.

Harvey said nothing. He couldn't say anything! The pain, embarrassment, and humility upon his face said more than words ever could. Harvey wanted to flee from the restaurant, then magically transport himself to the safe confines of his bedroom in Grangeford. There, he'd spend several hours (or days) hiding under his blankets until he found the will and courage to face the world ... or eventually face a slow, merciless, and horrible death.

"Goddamn!" laughed Dani. "For a moment I thought you faggots were serious!"

"Only in your dreams," snickered Billy Joe, turning toward Harvey. "Ain't that right, buddy?"

Harvey slouched in his chair and struggled to sip his water. Most of it spilled upon his shirt.

"In my worst day I can still trounce you in a shooting match," Billy Joe told Dani. "And this ain't my worst day."

"I wrote a new poem last week," Harvey said to Debra, intending to change the subject. "I'd give you a few stanzas, but you'll probably think it's stupid."

"You write poetry?" asked Debra, excitedly.

"Bullshit!" Dani cursed at Billy Joe. "A wetback like you can't hit the broad side of a shithouse!"

"Talk's cheap, loudmouth," said Billy Joe. "Once I'm done with you, you'll forget all about trap shooting and take up knitting."

"Sure," said Harvey, anxiously. "I take up knitting ... I mean, I write poetry!"

"I'd like to read it sometime," said Debra.

"By the time I kick your ass up over your shoulder blades," threatened Dani, "you won't be able to sit down for more than a week, Billy Joe Butthole!"

"You got an e-mail address I can send them to?" asked Harvey.

"What are they about?" asked Debra.

"Horseshit!" hollered Billy Joe. "You may think you're a good shot, but you can't pour piss out of a boot, even with the instructions on the heel!"

"What are they about?" asked Harvey, struggling to ignore Billy Joe and Dani. "Oh, one of my poems is about five-hundred words in length, and another is about six-hundred-and-fifty ..."

"That's not what I meant!" giggled Debra. "What are they about?"

"My ass!" bellowed Dani. "No contest, pal! By the end of the day, you'll be so butt-hurt you won't be able to take a leak without having it run down your little pink panties!"

"Hey, you two!" a voice shouted from the kitchen.

Seconds later, a heavy-set woman approached the teens' table. She wore a bright, violet dress. Her face and lips were smeared in make-up and gloss. "Can I ask you to keep it down to a dull roar?" she requested.

"Sorry, ma'am!" apologized Harvey. "I was only talking about ... Poetry."

"Not you!" the woman corrected, motioning toward Dani and Billy Joe. "You two. Keep it down ... please?"

"Sorry about all that," Debra said, diplomatically. "My friends get a little excited. I'll make sure they behave themselves. I promise!"

"Enjoy your breakfast," the heavyset woman said with an awkward smile. She turned and slowly returned to the kitchen.

"Nosy old whore," mumbled Dani. It didn't matter if she was a visitor or not. She wasn't about to letting a useless old hick telling her what to do! "I'd like to backhand her ugly-assed face into the mud."

"So," said Debra, thrilled to be in the company of a fellow writer. "Tell me more about your poetry."

Harvey debated on what to say. It didn't just involve his poetry, but various short stories, held in sheets of lined paper or hidden within a laptop computer. It would've been great to sit down for serious conversations concerning his work. Much of his poetry and prose involved his feelings and relationship toward guys ... mainly Billy Joe. Whether he chose to send this material to someone he hardly knew, such as Debra, well, that was debatable. In time, however, he had to share his work with everyone, even if it meant revealing secrets to those who had no business knowing them. This frightened Harvey. Was he gay? Yes! His love for Billy Joe proved as much. Was he prepared to openly identify himself as such?

Absolutely not!

"Can you e-mail me your manuscripts?" begged Debra. "I try to write, but I always get discouraged."

Harvey shrugged. He was obligated to share his work. This is what writers do, right? They give and take feedback. They risk criticism and rejection. They dare to reveal themselves. They show who they truly are and what they are, and pray not to get burned or experience heartbreak. If

Harvey did get serious about writing, then he had no choice but to give it to those who'd evaluate and critique it. Let it come back with enough red marks scrawled upon paper to appear as if someone bled to death. This was the price writers paid. They generally hated the process, and were too easily injured by it. But if risk and pain made the work better, then the process was worth it.

Right?

And, if Harvey's writing revealed a great deal about him, then wasn't that part of the gamble in the life of artists?

"Well, Harvey?" pressed Debra. "May I please read your poems? Please?"

"Okay," agreed Harvey, anxiously. "I can send them to you as soon as I get home tomorrow afternoon. You on Facebook or Twitter?"

Debra smiled. "Should I send you a friend request?"

"Sure!"

Debra fetched her cell phone from a purse, got on the free wi-fi furnished by the diner, and accessed her Facebook page. "What's your last name?" she asked.

"Madden." Harvey cleared his throat. "I'm listed by my name. Harvey Madden."

"Oh, there you are!" shouted Debra, happily. "And there you go. Mission accomplished. Sent you a friend request."

Harvey got on his own account, spotted Debra's request, and accepted it. "Looks like we're officially friends now!" he snickered.

After breakfast, Billy Joe and Dani went to their own vehicles to show off their firearms. On Halfway's Main Street, it wasn't unusual to publicly display guns. Harvey and Debra stood to one side, merely pretending to care.

Finally, Harvey had enough of Billy Joe and Dani's endless bragging and wanted to be alone. Although he barely knew his way around town, it was difficult to get lost in a community with so few streets and avenues, many of them dead ends. "When's the shooting contest start?" he inquired.

"Two," told Dani. "At the VFW, outside of town past the Fairgrounds."

"See ya there," said Harvey. "I think maybe Debra and I are just going to wander around and talk."

"Don't get lost," urged Billy Joe.

"In Halfway?" chuckled Harvey. "Don't worry, we won't venture too far off. Maybe I'll lay out bread crumbs as I walk, and hopefully a bird won't pluck them up."

"Make sure you don't run into a wicked old witch," commented Billy Joe. "Or you'll end up in the pot."

Harvey laughed. "Only if she's selling it!"

18

Harvey and Debra bought a couple of Hershey bars and Cokes at the Halfway Market, and casually strolled a few back streets. They chatted about music, movies, TV, books, and what they planned to do once they were on their own.

Harvey hoped to gain acceptance and appreciation as a writer. Secretly, he also wanted to be an advocate for gay and lesbian youth. When and if that time ever came, well, it was anyone's guess.

Harvey and Debra passed the Pine Eagle Clinic, then wandered into the Lions Club where they plopped down at a bench and table to relax. The sun was out, the traffic was light, and the setting relaxing and calm.

"When I finally make it big as a romantic novelist," spoke Debra, in a wishful and dreamy tone, "I plan to own a number of homes -- One in the Hollywood hills, a second in the south of France, and a third someplace in rural New England."

"That's not asking for too much, is it?" commented Harvey, sarcastically. "Think I'll just settle for a tiny cottage, far from the needs and expectations of others. Just a quiet little place where I don't have to get along with anyone but myself."

"Where do you want your cottage at? Ireland or Vermont?"

Harvey snickered. "Mars!"

"Oh, c'mon, you've never been to Mars!" giggled Debra. "What even makes you think the weather up there will agree with you?"

"It probably won't! But when was the last time you've been to the south of France or New England?"

"I've never been to those places," admitted Debra, frowning. "To be totally honest with you, Harvey, I haven't really been much of anywhere."

Harvey sought illumination.

"I hardly get out of Union County," explained Debra. "I've only been to Portland, once. And the farthest east I've ever been is to a fat aunt's house, in Laramie Wyoming." She shrugged. "Isn't much, is it?"

"That makes me feel kind of rotten," mumbled Harvey, thinking himself among the unworthy privileged. "When I was younger, my folks took me on trips all over the place."

"Such as?"

"Well." Harvey took time to think. "To begin with, we'd avoid places like Disney Land or Universal City. Too 'plastic' for Dad's taste. Instead, we'd go to art galleries, museums, jazz concerts, book signings." He smiled enthusiastically. "And, get this. Poetry readings! Tons of poetry readings!"

"That's awesome, Harvey! What other cool places?"

"Billy Joe wants to move to Nashville when he gets older. He's never been there, but I have been a bunch of times! Among my favorite spots there are the War Memorial, the Parthenon, and the Ryman Auditorium."

"I'm jealous." Debra shook her head in dismay. "You've been everywhere, and I've been nowhere."

"Well, I've never been to Sammyville. Not sure if I really wanna go."

"Don't," stated Debra, with utmost certainty. "You wouldn't like it. That place is scary!"

Don't worry. I'll take your word for it."

Debra slouched. She felt sick to her stomach and deflated, a pathetic version of what she wanted to be, verses who she really was. A timid, small-town girl with stars in her eyes, but with little or no knowledge of the outside world. Debra wanted to break free from her limited experiences and find the courage within herself to live life to the fullest. She questioned if that was even possible. The reality of her present situation agonized her no end.

Debra scooted closer to Harvey on the bench. Slowly, she reached out to run her fingers along his long, blonde locks. "Anyone ever tell you that you got the nicest hair?" she mumbled, in a slightly seductive tone.

"My mom, on several occasions," responded Harvey, fearing what Debra had in mind. It was one thing to be her friend, a fellow artist to give or receive feedback for words scrawled upon lined paper. But Debra's actions and behavior told Harvey that she wanted more from him, which he wasn't willing or able to give out.

Debra crossed the line when she placed her hand on Harvey's bare thigh, just above the knee.

Harvey swiftly pulled away from Debra, in shock and anger. The expression in his eyes warned of potential fireworks.

"I'm so sorry!" apologized Debra, her voice high-pitched and frightened.

Now Harvey felt a need to apologize. He didn't mean to react so harshly. The situation grew tense and awkward.

"I'm sorry, Harvey!" repeated Debra, nervously. "I ... I don't know how to explain this, but ... Well ... it's just that ... you're my idea of what I always imagined my own version of Prince Charming to be!"

"Me?" voiced Harvey, in disbelief and self-deprecating humor. "I'm your idea of 'Prince Charming'?"

Debra nodded 'yes'.

Harvey rolled his eyes back and sighed. His face altered to a violet blush. "I'm far from anyone's idea of 'Prince Charming'! I'm too short, too scrawny, and too dorky to be Prince Charming!"

"You're wrong! Believe me, I think you're one of the most handsome guys I ever met! I ... I ... I think you're perfect!"

Harvey snickered.

"I mean it," claimed Debra. "I think you're one of the cutest guys I ever met!"

Harvey laughed. "You have really bad taste in men!"

"No, Harvey! You're cute! Handsome, charming, and cute! Not only that, but you're really smart!"

Harvey took in a deep breath. He remained oddly flattered, yet still embarrassed and even hostile in the manner which Debra tried coming onto him.

"You overrate me," he said. "Look, I'm just this goofy kid from a hick college town in a hick corner of Oregon."

"Maybe you don't belong in a hick town," suggested Debra. "How many kids in Grangeford read T.S. Eliot, Walt Whitman or Robert Browning, or listen to Bach, Beethoven, or Mozart?"

"You got a point there."

"I'm sorry," whined Debra, sadly. "I don't know. Guess I was just hoping we could get together more often ... Talk books, TV, movies. Talk about what we're gonna do when we're no longer living with Mommy and Daddy." She looked deeply into Harvey's eyes, and fought the urge to weep. "The guys around my school don't take an interest in me. You've been so nice and wanted to hang out."

"You're a nice person, Deb. And I hope someday a guy does take an interest in you, and is your 'Prince Charming'. I'm just not the guy." Harvey sighed. "The truth is, I'm taken. The whole point of going on this trip is that the person I'm ... me and the person I'm with can have some time together."

"I didn't know there was someone else with you! The only one I've ever seen you with is Billy Joe. If there's a girl or something hanging out with you guys, then why isn't she here with ...?"

"I'm gay!" Harvey blurted out, unaware of it until the words had spilled from his mouth.

There was a deathly silence. Debra's jaw dropped open as her eyes widened. "You're ... you're gay?" she gasped.

"I ... I ... meant ..." Harvey stammered, struggling yet failing to claim he had misspoken. "I mean ... I meant ... I'm not ... Y' know, what I just ..."

"You? You're gay?" repeated Debra, wondering if she had heard him correctly.

It was no use. Harvey grew tongue-tied, and the words refused to come. His fiery blush, sweating palms and forehead, and jittery speech gave him away.

"You're gay?" Debra whispered. "You're gay?"

Harvey inadvertently began to laugh, frightened by the consequences of his actions. Strangely, he also felt free and liberated, as if to turn yet another key to unlock the doors and chains of a self-imposed prison. He didn't laugh out of humor. He simply couldn't help it!

Okay. Debra now knew more about Harvey than what either of them had expected. Okay, so what the hell? How much of that could she pose against him? That little shrimp likely couldn't hurt a fly! That was, unless she told everyone and their dog that Harvey liked guys ... then it'd evolve into be a totally different story altogether!

"I'm gay," mumbled Harvey, as if to disclose a terrible and painful secret. It was a relief to get it out. Yet, there were noticeable hints of shame. "Yeah, Debra ... I ... I'm gay."

Debra sought knowledge and clarification, while Harvey begged for understanding and acceptance.

"I didn't plan to say anything ..." Harvey shook his head. "But it just kinda came out, and ..."

"You and Billy Joe?" asked Debra, in sympathy and support.

Harvey nodded his head, 'yes'.

"It's okay!" laughed Debra. Trust me, it's okay. You're safe with me!"

"It's just that ..." mumbled Harvey. "Look, I ... I knew since the sixth grade, or at least I suspected ..."

"It's okay, Harvey. I had no idea! But now that you told me, it's all good!"

Harvey wiped away a teardrop, then gave Debra an awkward grin.

"So, it's you and Billy Joe?" chuckled Debra.

"Yeah." Harvey wondered what he had gotten himself into. "Me and Billy Joe."

Debra smirked.

"What?" snickered Harvey, his face beet-red. "What's so funny?"

"Forgive me for saying this, but I never imagined you hooking up with ... well, with Billy Joe."

"Why not?" questioned Harvey, defensively.

Debra hesitated. "You seem so refined and clean, so well-educated and articulate and, well ... Billy Joe's real folksy and kind of a hayseed."

"A hayseed?"

"Well, just look at him! All right. 'Hayseed' seems a bit strong. What about ... 'Small-town-ish'?"

"Look," sighed Harvey. "He may be folksy, and a hick, and a hayseed. Or a hillbilly, or a 'good old boy'. Or an ignorant slob. But I love Billy Joe, and for what it's worth, he loves me. I hope to spend the rest of my life with him. It's all that matters to me!"

"It's okay. Trust me, it's okay. I'm sorry. It's just that ... Guess I'm feeling jealous and jilted right now."

"What do you mean?"

"I thought that I found my 'Prince Charming' in you, and I guess it's not to be. I'm really sorry! I still think that you're really cute, and I'm hurt that we can be nothing more than friends!"

"I hope you do find your 'Prince Charming'." Harvey gave Debra a gentle kiss on the forehead. "But whether anyone understands or not, well ... I guess I'm Billy Joe's 'Prince Charming', and he's mine. I don't like that stupid mustache, and I absolutely hate his damned dog. But, no matter what, I love Billy Joe, more than anything! And, for what it's worth, he's still my 'Prince Charming', which means ... I'm his 'Prince Charming'."

19

Harvey and Debra stopped by Buffalo Bills for hamburgers and Cokes. By now, Billy Joe and Dani were already at the local VFW, preparing for the shooting contest.

After lunch, Harvey and Debra wandered to the VFW, a short walk out of town beyond the Baker County Fairgrounds. The parking lot was filled with several vehicles. Cars lined both sides of a narrow, black-top highway adjacent the VFW, and traffic had slowed.

Harvey took note of the various bumper stickers promoting Republican candidates, NRA stickers, and those seeking to Make America Great Again. Many participants were open in their support of Donald Trump, former Second Congressional Representative Greg Walden, and other conservative candidates and causes.

Harvey rolled his eyes back, took in a deep breath, and sighed. He felt like someone daring to enter a hostile territory. He vowed to remain civil, keep his mouth shut when it came to politics and religion, and go along to get along.

Harvey and Debra spotted Billy Joe and Dani sitting together in the shade of the VFW Hall. Both held unloaded 12-guage shotguns in their arms. Harvey smiled and offered a pleasant greeting.

"Wondering when you'd get here," grunted Billy Joe. "Thinking you might not be here to cheer me on."

"I wouldn't miss it in the world," spoke Harvey, sarcastically.

Billy Joe stepped toward a small table to pay an entrance fee. An attractive, middle-aged woman took down participants' names and worked a cash register. Money raised in this event would help a local family get back on its feet, after a devastating house fire.

"Name, please," the woman requested, pen and paper in hand.

"Billy Joe McBain." He reached into his wallet for some cash. "But you can call me … Utah."

"Terrific!" the woman cheered. "I've been a member of the LDS Church all my life!"

Billy Joe scratched his head. "Excuse me, ma'am?"

"Are you a Mormon, too?" the woman asked.

"Uh … No," Billy Joe mumbled. "Me, I'm a … a Buddhist. Me and my family … We're all … Buddhists …"

Billy Joe paid the entrance fee, then wandered away with an awkward look on his face.

"So, how many Buddhists are there in your family?" asked Harvey. "I'm sure your grandparents will like that. And if you don't mind my asking … What're we gonna do with a turkey or a ham if you win one? Give it to Corky?"

Billy Joe frowned.

Harvey glanced out over the growing crowd to see Cliff Walker, leaning on a cane. Cliff had a cigarette hanging from one side of his mouth, his bottom lip filled with Copenhagen.

"Hey, thanks for the bike," Harvey said as he approached Cliff.

"Knew that'd put a smile on yer face," said Cliff, with a tobacco-stained grin. "Reckon a bike's gotta beat stickin' yer thumbs out f'r a ride t' school 'r work."

"Sure does. It'll make life so much easier. Thanks! You have no idea how much it means to me!"

"Yer welcome." Cliff checked his watch. "Say, partner, you wanna run out t' the rig and fetch my .06 and 4-10?"

"Sure thing." Harvey sprinted to Cliff's woodcutting truck for the firearms, which rested on gun racks in the back window.

"You ain't shootin' today?" asked Cliff, rubbing dust away from his 30.06.

"Naw."

Cliff eyed Harvey, in suspicion. "How come?"

"Mom and Dad never wanted me to get into guns and hunting," explained Harvey. "They're peace-loving, tree-hugging, save-the-whale types."

"You ain't like that, are ya?"

"Billy Joe takes me out shooting once in a while. My folks won't let me own a gun. Billy Joe forgot more about guns than I'll ever know. I don't really like them that much, but I'm not trying to take them away from law-abiding citizens, or anything like that." Harvey cleared his throat, hoping not to anger Cliff. "They're just not my cup of tea, that's all."

"Good deal. Thinkin' I might have t' take the goddamn bike back."

"Please don't!" laughed Harvey. "I like it too much!"

"Just keep the gears good and greased an' tires filled with air. Bike'll last ya a good long while."

"Are you competing today?"

"Trap shootin' and rifle contest."

"You're going up against Billy Joe," said Harvey. "Don't let him know it, but I hope you beat him. He's my … My best friend, but he's awfully cocky and needs to be put in his place." He pointed at Billy Joe and Dani. "Him and that girl in the cut-offs. Do me a favor and show them both who's boss!"

Cliff smiled. "I'll give 'em hell, Harve!"

Seconds later, the same woman who thought that Billy Joe was a Mormon fetched a portable microphone from the table and welcomed everyone to the charitable event. "Awesome!" she exclaimed, revealing thick layers of lipstick. "We've got a super turn-out today! This benefit is to help the Endicott family get back on their feet, after their house caught fire back in May. Dale and Janice and their three kids have lost almost everything, and they've worked really hard to rebuild and start over. Thanks everyone for showing up today, to help these great folks out!"

A round of applause swept through the crowd, along with a few jokes, gentle ribbing, and laughter.

"This is a family gathering," the woman continued. "Keep the rough language down, and be good sports. Remember, we're here to help the Endicotts. It doesn't matter who wins or loses, because the only winners are Dale and Janice! Above all else, remember that guns and booze don't go together. No drinking till after the shooting stops!"

Once again, this was followed by ill-jokes, kidding around, and giggles.

"Before we begin,'" the woman concluded. "I'd like to introduce you … As if they need any introduction … I'd like to introduce you to the recipients of this event." The woman turned to Dale and Janice, who stood nervously to one side. "C'mon, you two! Don't be shy! C'mon over and say 'hi'!"

Dale shook his head 'no', and blushed. A nervous chuckle slipped from his mouth. Janice was also apprehensive, but reluctantly pushed her husband to the microphone. Onlookers heckled and chided the Endicotts, who were apparently well-loved and respected in town.

"You folks care to say anything?" the woman asked, handing the microphone to Janice since Dale refused to touch it. "C'mon, we're here for you!"

Janice took the microphone to thank the VFW, and those who did what they could to help her family through what proved to be a very trying period. Along with the shooting competition, pies, pastries and cakes to be auctioned off. A great deal of effort had been put in to assist Dale, Janice, and their three children.

After crowding themselves into a neighbor's bedroom for the past few weeks, the Endicotts had found a small house to rent, and were excited to move in.

Dale and Janice were in their early thirties. They were high school sweethearts, and got married soon after graduation. Initially, the couple located to Boise where Dale took a job with Idaho Power and Janice became a cashier at an Albertsons. The two oldest kids, Dale Jr. and Andi, were born in St. Alphonsus Regional Medical Center, while the third, Bobbi, was born in Baker City. The Endicotts moved back to their hometown in Halfway, where Dale worked at Brownlee, Oxbow, and Hells Canyon Dams on the Snake River, and Janice a part-time cashier at the Old Pine Market.

Dale was a tall, lanky fellow, and resembled various leading men in western movies or TV shows from the Forties or Fifties. Janice was a short, squat woman with fiery red hair and a freckled face. Their three kids ranged from ages twelve to seven and, like their mother, were gingers.

As her throat tightened and speech grew jittery, Janice voiced a tearful gratitude to those who had afforded her family love, kindness, and support.

The competition now started, with a few rounds of pistol, black powder, and rifle competitions. Billy Joe took the time to clean and maintain his twelve-gauge. He smiled eagerly and confidently, as Harvey wished him well.

"Thanks, Harve," acknowledged Billy Joe. "Gonna do my best, though I think I got a good chance of winning."

"You're going up against Cliff," informed Harvey.

"Cliff? The old guy we cut wood for yesterday?"

Harvey cleared his throat and nodded 'yes'. "Look, I know it'll shatter your ego," he whispered, cautiously, "but why don't you let him win?"

"What the hell?"

"Let Cliff win," urged Harvey. "After all, he's a nice guy, and he did give me the bike."

"Yeah, but ..."

"It'll mean a lot to him. I mean, him living alone and feeling lonely and sad, after losing his wife and everything."

Billy Joe frowned.

"It's like what the lady said," added Harvey. "This isn't for our sake, but to help the Endicotts."

"Well, maybe letting Cliff win might be the right thing. But it ain't Cliff I'm worried about. It's Dani."

"Dani?"

"Yeah," said Billy Joe, anxiously. "She's been saying all day how she's gonna beat my ass."

"Figures."

"There's always a lotta loud talk, boasting, and bragging at these events. Hell, I'm just as bad. But I think Dani means it. If she loses, she'll be mad as all hell and go around blaming everyone over it, including God. She'll get downright mean, and holler at me simply because she can. I'll be damned if I'm gonna let her win."

Harvey snickered.

"Something else about her that bothers me," admitted Billy Joe. "Pretty sure she wants to get in my drawers."

Harvey rolled his eyes back.

"She's been acting all friendly and nicey-nice and hornier than a toad when she's not reminding me how bad she's gonna kick my ass," said Billy Joe. "I ain't sure if she learned her lousy behavior from somebody else, or was born that way. One thing's for sure. She ain't someone I care to know all that well. She's got something bad wrong with her."

"You got that right," agreed Harvey, sighing in relief to learn that Billy Joe had no interest in Dani, whatsoever. "Debra tried to get friendly with me, too. But I ... talked her out of it."

"How?"

Harvey hesitated.

"Aw, c'mon, tell me!" begged Billy Joe. "How'd you 'talk her outa it'?"

Harvey bit his bottom lip. "I accidentally told her the truth ... About us."

Billy Joe groaned.

"I didn't mean to!" cried Harvey. "It just ... came out, that's all ... Look, it's hard to explain ..."

"Well, ain't that good to know? I'll be goddamned-go-to-hell over it!"

"I'm sorry! It just ... slipped out."

Billy Joe gritted his teeth. Moments passed before he rubbed his chin, shrugged, and pasted on a phony smile. "Aw, well, what the hell? We'll be outa here first thing tomorrow morning. Who cares what folks around here think about us? Even if they do find out, it might be a big deal until they find something else to gossip over the back fence about."

With that, Billy Joe took a deep breath, tucked on his shirt, and took his place in the trap shoot.

<h1 style="text-align:center">20</h1>

Five contestants took part in the trap shoot competition. Along with Billy Joe, Cliff, and Dani, there was a twelve-year-old, towheaded boy and a local fellow with bad teeth, an unshaven face, dirty clothes, and a foul odor.

Billy Joe shook his opponents' hands and wished them well. He took a strong interest in the twelve-year-old kid, who was very conscientious of firearm safety. This was apparent in the manner the boy handled his shotgun, by keeping it pointed toward the ground in front of him and away from others. Based upon conversations between the boy and his father, goofing off with guns was a "sin", never to be tolerated. By his father's insistence, the boy wore yellow-tinted safety glasses and earplugs.

"Billy Joe McBain," he introduced himself to the twelve-year-old. "But you can call me ..." Billy Joe shot a comical glance toward Harvey. "Aw, just call me 'Bill'."

"Kyle Anderson," the boy responded, thrilled that Billy Joe treated him as an equal. He motioned toward his father. "That's my dad, Josh Anderson. We're from Prairie City."

"Glad to make your acquaintance," spoke Josh, a big man with a face seemingly carved from granite, along with dishwater hair that grayed at the temples. "We been fishing on the Imnaha when we got wind of these doings, and decided to throw in."

"Great day for it!" said Billy Joe. "Well, good luck, Kyle. Something tells me you're gonna be a handful. Think I better keep my eyes on you!"

He gave Kyle a gentle nudge on the shoulder. "Y' might just beat me today."

"Well, I'll try," answered Kyle, with a bashful grin. "I guess."

"Aw, you'll do a'right," commented Billy Joe, once again shaking Kyle's hand. "Good luck to ya!"

Cliff was chosen as leader of the trap shoot competition. Along with taking the number one position on the firing line, it was his job to inspect the clay pigeons.

Cliff fetched two clay pigeons from a large cardboard box, then carefully measured them in both hands. The clay pigeons were round, yellow and orange cylinders, four-and-a-half inches in diameter and nearly three-and-a half ounces in weight. Cliff looked the clay pigeons up one side and down the other, to make sure they were "up to snuff."

Cliff declared that the clay pigeons were "good enough f'r his likin'." He then ordered the other contestants to take their places.

Cliff took the first position, Billy Joe the second, Kyle the third, Dani was fourth, and the guy with a dirty clothes and pungent smell the fifth. Each contestant got five shots per round, and scores were based on the number of targets hit. Contestants changed positions on the firing line for reach round. The contestant to strike the highest number of clay pigeons in the match was the winner.

Cliff went up first. He allowed his targets to gain altitude before shooting, but still managed to blow all five out of the sky.

Cheers for the old widower.

Billy Joe was next. He eagerly and immediately nailed every one of his targets, within a second or two after they had left the thrower.

Words of praise and applause for the cart pusher.

Kyle was next. He was regarded as an underdog and a crowd favorite. Awkwardly, he turned to Josh.

"Go ahead, Kyle," urged Josh, softly. "Just do your best. That's all I can ask of you."

Kyle made contact with three of his first four clay pigeons. He had missed his fourth pigeon, but only managed to nick his fifth. Still, it wasn't a bad performance, and gained tremendous support and admiration from the crowd.

Dani was conscious of the large number of young men who eyed her tanned legs and long, blonde hair. She took her place on the firing line, with an obsessive drive to "thump Billy Joe's ass". Crying "Pull!" in a high-pitched, shrill command, she successfully scored on all five of her clay pigeons.

The fifth competitor, regarded as a town drunk, Ne'er-do-well, and freeloader, missed all of his targets by a mile and gained no support from anyone.

The second round proved more challenging than the first. As before, Billy Joe and Dani hit each and every one their marks. Kyle came very close, but missed two of his five targets. Once again, Cliff took his own sweet time, yet nailed his pigeons. The town drunk, who couldn't shoot straight still failed to shoot straight, and missed every one of his targets.

After blowing the second round, the town drunk reached into one pocket for a flask filled with some cheap rotgut, and took a sip.

Since alcoholic beverages were strictly forbidden, the drunk was eliminated from the competition. If that wasn't bad enough, he created a scene by screaming, hollering, and cursing while being forcibly ejected out of the game. Moments, later, he found comfort and solace in a bottle of tequila, located on the floorboard of his beat-up AMC Gremlin.

Quietly, Billy Joe called Kyle to his side. "You're doing real good," he spoke, resting one hand on the boy's shoulder. "But you gotta lead your target a bit more."

Kyle shrugged, unsure of what Billy Joe had told him.

"Instead of aiming right straight at the target," explained Billy Joe, "place your bead a few yards ahead, then fire."

"How come?" asked Kyle, turning toward Josh for reinforcement.

"Trust me," Billy Joe went on. "Aim slightly ahead of your target, and chances are you'll nail it."

Josh nodded in agreement.

"Relax," chuckled Billy Joe. "You act like you're more scared of missing your targets, than you are excited in hitting 'em. C'mon ... relax. You're doing real good. Calm down, take your time, and have fun. You can only get better and, trust me, you will!"

Kyle graciously accepted the advice, then returned to his place on the firing line. Cliff gave Billy Joe a thumbs-up for helping the boy out.

"Nothing like picking favorites," Dani griped at Billy Joe. "What's your problem? You think I got herpes, or what?"

Billy Joe merely smiled but said nothing.

The third round went well for Billy Joe, Cliff, and Kyle, but not for Dani. The three men hit all of their targets, but Dani missed two of hers.

Rather than taking her failure in stride, Dani cursed under her breath or blamed the wind, the sun being in her eyes, or given "lopsided and wobbly pigeons".

Dani's conduct caused her to lose favor from the crowd, for the exception on a few guys who stared endlessly at her long, blonde hair, shapely figure, and well-tanned legs.

By the end of the fifth round, Billy Joe and Cliff earned perfect scores by hitting all twenty-five of their targets, and entered a championship round. It was decided that the first competitor to miss his target would be eliminated, leaving the remaining player as the victor. Billy Joe and Cliff agreed to his arrangement, and shook hands.

Kyle won over many warm hearts, kind words, and tremendous support, despite having to leave the competition. Even then, he was disheartened by his "lousy showing". His watery eyes and hurt expressions made him that much more of a sympathetic figure. Kyle was his own harshest critic, though everyone assured him that he did well.

"I love you, son," Josh said, giving Kyle a hug.

"Next time we need up, reckon you might just beat me," Billy Joe told Kyle, patting his back.

With that, Kyle and Josh sat down with soft drinks, a burger, and fries which they bought at a concession stand. They had a chance to discuss everything Kyle did right that day and, with practice, how he'd gradually improve.

Despite her claims that the match was rigged, Dani gained scant applause and support from onlookers. Whispering, she told Billy Joe to do something which is physically impossible. Dani retreated to Debra's small car, where she refused to speak to anyone.

It proved to be a long, hard match. Billy Joe and Cliff managed to score for every round. The audience looked on with extreme anticipation and suspense. Eventually, one player would meet a painful and excruciating defeat. Still, the way both men were shooting, everyone wondered if the contest would end in a draw.

At some point, Billy Joe and Cliff took a breather in order to relax and hydrate.

"Remember what I told you," Harvey whispered in Billy Joe's ear.

"What?" asked Billy Joe, sipping a can of lukewarm Pepsi.

"Let Cliff win."

"You asking me to throw the match?"

"Try not to make it look too obvious," suggested Harvey, with a sly grin.

"But ... What the hell for?"

"It'll mean a lot to him."

"If I let him win," sighed Billy Joe. "The ways things are going, he might just beat me, fair and square."

"Please?"

"Nothing like guilt-trippin' me, y' jerk."

Harvey chuckled. "It'll make you feel better."

"That's what you think." Billy Joe wandered back to the firing line, in anger and frustration.

Harvey remained in the shade of the VFW Hall, enjoying a cool breeze and wondering if Billy Joe would go along with the plan.

Billy Joe was passionate about firearms and hunting. He spent much of his time at gun ranges to improve his marksmanship. He loved the outdoors, and often bagged deer and elk on the first day of the season. He also loved backpacking and fishing. He dreamed of eventually owning a remote cabin in the middle of nowhere, with no electricity or indoor plumbing, and roughing it.

In truth, Cliff was likely better with firearms than Billy Joe and, as far as anyone knew, could have easily "smoked" him. With that in mind, would Billy Joe simply allow Cliff to win? Or would Cliff grow weary of the contest, and give in to Billy Joe?

After a coin toss, Cliff took the first shot, and blew his target to Kingdom Come. Billy Joe also made contact with his clay pigeon.

As the audience responded with enthusiastic applause, Billy Joe gave Harvey a snotty and defiant grin.

Harvey frowned.

The next round went the same. Cliff took a little more time to hit his target, but did so squarely. Billy Joe shouted, "Pull!" as his clay pigeon left the thrower. Leisurely, as if to take no interest or care in the outcome. Eventually he aimed, pulled the trigger ...

... And blew his target out of the sky.

Once again, he gave Harvey a knowing grin. Harvey rolled his eyes back and sighed.

Next, Cliff managed only to nick a small corner from his clay pigeon as it flew, awkwardly away. Still, this was regarded as a successful hit, and kept him in the game.

Billy Joe swallowed in a deep breath, placed the twelve-gauge to his shoulder, and yelled, "Pull!"

The target escaped from the thrower ...

Billy Joe pulled the trigger ...

And missed by a mile!

The crowd reacted with oohs, 'ahhs', surprise, shock, painful resignation, and finally applause.

"Thanks," Billy Joe spoke quietly as he shook Cliff's hand. "It sure was a kick in the ass, but you whooped me up one side and down the other."

Cliff said nothing. He simply gave Billy Joe an angry stare, then grunted.

With that, Billy Joe slowly wandered back toward Harvey.

Harvey jumped to his feet and embraced Billy Joe.

"Happy now, y' miserable little bastard?" Billy Joe whispered in Harvey's ear. "Got my ass beat on account of you!"

21

Less than two hours after the trap competition, the charity event was over. Winners were announced, trophies were awarded, and the Endicotts were handed a small-yet-well-appreciated check.

Despite being an outsider, Billy Joe became a fan favorite to locals, due to his obvious skills. Most everyone marveled at his marksmanship and sportsmanlike conduct. When and if the community ever staged another shooting contest, he'd surely be invited.

Harvey and Billy Joe hopped in the GMC then gassed up at the Co-Op, near the edge of town.

No sooner had Billy Joe filled his tank, Debra and Dani pulled into the service station in the VW. Dani hopped out of the passenger side and quickly approached Billy Joe. "We're on our way over to Buffalo Bills," she said. "Wondering if you two losers might wanna join us."

"How come?" snickered Billy Joe. "So you can remind me and everyone else how the wind got in your eyes, or that the sun blew so bad you couldn't hit nothin'?"

"No," answered Dani, wearing a labored grin to conceal her aggravation and animosity. "Just wanting to know if you're still as queer for Harvey the Boy Wonder as you were for that snotnosed runt from Prairie City?"

Harvey rolled his eye back and sighed.

"Just tryna be a good-ol'-boy to a fellow shooter, that's all," informed Billy Joe. "Kyle might not be all that great, yet. Few years from now, watch out. He might almost be as good as I am. By this time next week, he'll be whoopin' your ass up one side and down the other."

"In your wildest dreams, smartass."

Billy Joe hung the gas nozzle up, then used his debit card. "Just to show I ain't picking no favors, I thought you done a'right, too." He shook Dani's hand. "Even if the sun and the wind and God was up against you."

"And just to show I don't hold grudges," said Dani, "I'd like to buy you and your bed-buddy a cup of coffee."

"Whadda ya think?" Billy Joe asked Harvey, poking his head through the driver's side window. "Wanna head on over for to Buffalo Bills, just to shoot the shit?"

"I told Angela we'd have dinner with them tonight," said Harvey. Although he would've enjoyed chatting with Debra, the last thing he wanted was to spend another second around Dani.

Although he got the hint, Billy Joe wasn't one to refuse a cup of Joe, even from a competitor. "I'm looking forward to doing a bit of pickin' and grinnin' with Barb, myself," he said, diplomatically. "C'mon, let's stop by for a spell, then mosey on up to camp. How 'bout it?"

"I guess," answered Harvey, tiredly.

"Reckon we'll head over for a bit," Billy Joe told Dani. "Meet'cha over there."

Moments later, Billy Joe pulled in across Main Street from Buffalo Bills. Debra's VW was already there. The two girls were inside, awaiting Harvey and Billy Joe's arrival.

Billy Joe placed the GMC in PARK and shut off the ignition. He glanced over at Harvey, who was clearly displeased about spending time with the likes of Dani. "Do we really have to go in there?" voiced Harvey. He felt exhausted by the endless sounds of gunfire, and sought only kind words along with the peace and quiet of Mother Nature.

"My folks ain't ones to turn down an invite from anyone," answered Billy, slapping Harvey's knee. "They raised me to be the same way. C'mon. Let's pop in, act like we're having a good time, then head up to the lake." He chuckled, wickedly. "Unless you wanna just sit here like a pouty little bitch and refuse another bitch's hospitality."

"Asshole," whispered Harvey, as he and Billy Joe wandered into the diner.

Already, there was a good number of people inside, and most of them let out shouts of celebration at Billy Joe. It was as if a celebrity had wandered through the restaurant's door.

Happily, Billy Joe milked the occasion by the shaking of hands along with enjoying a few comments on his showmanship during the competition. Slowly he worked his way through the various tables and well-wishers as Harvey reluctantly followed behind.

It seemingly took forever to reach Debra and Dani's table.

Debra remained polite and cordial as she chatted with Harvey. Even then, Harvey grew anxious, knowing she was aware of his relationship with Billy Joe. While she didn't pose a threat, an idle tongue just might. The last thing Harvey wanted or needed was to have Debra tell Dani a thing or two about the guys.

Billy Joe carried on with his good-old-boy, goat-roping, ranch-handing, cattle-punching façade. This, even if Dani began the conversation with the riddle, "How does a black girl know she's pregnant? If she pulls her tampon out and the cotton's been picked!"

Harvey barely contained his hatred toward Dani. Still, he didn't wish to make a scene. Instead, he chose to concentrate on discussing his favorite old books ... 'Catcher in the Rye', 'The Chocolate War', 'A Princess of Mars', and 'The Hobbit'. He wasn't at all interested in hearing about the shotgun competition, or anything else involving firearms. More than anything, he only wanted to return to camp, take a refreshing bath in the lake, then enjoy the remains of the day with hotdogs, salad, s'mores, and pleasant company.

Just when things seemingly couldn't get worse, Dani asked Billy Joe, "What's brown and green and yellow in between?"

Billy Joe didn't know the answer. After a long period of silence, he turned toward Dani as if to say, I dunno ... What?

Dani roared in laughter, "A nigger shitting in the grass!"

"What gives you the right to make sick racist jokes?" questioned Harvey, his face red from anger. "And just what the hell gives you a right to tell the whole world how much you despise people who aren't like you?"

The table grew deathly quiet, as Dani glared menacingly at Harvey.

"All right," continued Harvey, growing increasingly emotional and shrill. "You don't like blacks or Mexicans or gays. Why should I or anyone else have to put up with it? Or pretend that we're not offended? Or ... Or pretend that we're supposed to just sit here and go along with it?"

"Harvey ..." mumbled Billy Joe, nervously.

"Well, I suppose not everyone cares for racial humor," said Debra, diplomatically. "From what I gather from Harvey, his views are considerably more progressive than Dani's."

"I have as much right to my opinion as you do," argued Dani. "You idiotic, cry-baby liberals are all the same. So sanctimonious, so sensitive, so self-righteous and so holier-than-thou, so full of themselves, and so full of shit. Thinking you gotta open your mouths about anything and everything, even when you're totally clueless. So easily offended and put-off if others dare to speak their minds, or even make a harmless little joke!"

"At least I don't go around using words like 'spic' or 'faggots' or 'niggers'!" shouted Harvey, loud enough for others to hear. "Maybe you think you're some kind of comedian, but I sure as hell don't!"

"Then why don't you just take your nigger-loving, gun-grabbing ass outside?" snapped Dani. "Get out of here, before I throw you through the window!"

Debra released an awkward snicker.

"You wanna fight, bitch?" yelled Harvey, his voice quivering. "Fine! Let's go outside, so I can slap you into the middle of next week!"

"Oh, brother," whispered Billy Joe.

A couple of servers, a dishwasher, and a cook left the kitchen. Several patrons stepped from the adjoining tavern, to see what the commotion was all about. Restaurant customers looked on, in wonder and worry. Meanwhile, a couple of younger boys hoped they'd witness a brawl.

"I'm gonna beat your scrawny, little Commie ass into the ground!" threatened Dani. "Let's go outside where I'll do it!"

"Simmer down!" a voice called out from the kitchen. "If you're gonna fight, get as far away from here so it doesn't involve us!"

Billy Joe and Debra expected a human freight train to storm from the kitchen, based upon the low, loud, and intimidating command.

No matter how upset Harvey may have been, he now suffered an unbearable sense of shame, humiliation, and guilt. Seconds before, he wanted to clean Dani's clock. Now he hoped to apologize to everyone in Buffalo Bills, then slither away from everyone's sight and harsh judgments. He regarded himself as a fool, and knew better than to make a spectacle. He imagined his head getting ripped off, not by Dani, but from whoever or whatever exited the kitchen.

Based upon the explosive tone of the voice which issued an order to "simmer down", Harvey visualized some huge, slightly gray-haired old gal who'd been waiting tables since the dawn of man ... one who referred to patrons as "sweetheart", "darling", or "honey" ... someone who was compassionate one moment, then hard as nails the next ... someone unwilling to take crap from anybody.

So, if Harvey and Dani didn't straighten up and fly right, the Wrath of God would soon be upon them.

What stepped from the kitchen was a small-statured woman of about sixty. The woman had red, dyed hair, a tight-fitting, white sweatshirt, sneakers, and shorts which revealed two stocky, tanned legs. Despite the touch of gray at the temples, along with wrinkles on the forehead and under both eyes, there was a fierceness and determination in her.

Whether the woman frightened Dani, she gave Harvey reason to shutter. Harvey surmised that the woman had been in her share of scrapes, and won all of them. It wasn't a fear of getting hurt which troubled him. He presented himself to the people of Halfway in a childish and unappealing way. He gave them something to remember him for, which wasn't especially wholesome or good. He expected more from himself, and didn't come off as smart, honorable, or decent.

What could he do now to make an amends?

"You want some of it?" Dani challenged the woman.

Billy Joe and Debra urgently stepped between Dani and the woman.

Dani made no effort to fight her way through Billy Joe and Debra. Even then, she wanted to make a good show of it and pretend not to be afraid. "You wanna taste of my five knuckles?" Dani screamed out at the older woman. "Wouldn't take much to whip your wrinkled, ugly old ass!"

Harvey rolled his eyes back and sighed. The scene may have been oddly humorous, from the expressions on the faces of shocked witnesses. It was also pathetic, ridiculous, and useless. He realized that he'd remain a part of the community's collective memory. Nothing said he had to hang around and make things worse.

Harvey looked at the older woman. It was obvious that she wasn't happy with him. This only augmented his feelings of idiocy and inferiority. He tried to voice a simple "I'm sorry". It came out as a whimper.

Unable to say what he desperately wished to get out, Harvey sprinted to the door, ran outside, and beat a hasty retreat to the GMC.

Harvey heard Dani shrieking from inside Buffalo Bills. He didn't care. All he wanted was to return to Fish Lake and forget the whole affair.

Harvey got in the GMC's passenger side, and slammed the door behind him. He buried his face under both hands, took a deep breath, and struggled to slow his racing heart. He remained furious, extremely furious at Dani. At the same time, he doubted if he came off as any better.

Harvey sat in the truck and waited impatiently for Billy Joe. He was split between laughing at himself, or weeping in despair. He was at odds, and questioned if it was best to stomp Dani's guts in or keep his damned mouth shut.

Seconds later, Billy Joe stepped of Buffalo Bills with Debra and Dani. Without saying a word, Dani fled to the VW as Billy Joe and Debra talked amongst themselves. Harvey looked on, wondering what they were talking about, and already knew the answer.

Billy Joe crossed the street, hopped into the GMC, and turned over the ignition.

"What?" demanded Harvey.

"Looks like we ain't invited back in there for quite some while," cackled Billy Joe. "Well, they might let me go in, but I'm pretty sure you been 86'd for life."

Harvey lowered his head.

"Too bad," added Billy Joe. "Had you and Dani not got into that heated exchange, I mighta got me a free burger. First you beg me to throw the trap shoot, and now this. Thanks, Harve. Thanks a lot."

"Sorry," whispered Harvey.

"Aw hell, it's a'right. Dani had it coming, and I reckon you had to be the one to give it to her."

"I dunno about that."

"Aw, sure you did." Billy Joe slapped Harvey's knee. "You had to stick up for what you believe in and, boy, you sure did. I'm proud of you, even if we both got the boot."

"I feel so stupid," moped Harvey.

"Aw, you ain't stupid. You got your convictions, which means you can't keep your mouth shut when someone gets you all riled up." Billy Joe chuckled. "You can't help it if you ain't nothin' more than a nigger-lovin', gun-grabbin', Commie asshole faggot ..."

22

It was nearing evening once Harvey and Billy Joe returned to camp. Both were tired, sweaty, and in need of a bath. The two boys got into cut-off jeans and jumped in the lake. A pleasant breeze swept over the mountains.

Despite a chill in the air, Harvey and Billy Joe found the experience to be sobering and refreshing. Harvey, in particular, needed a chance to wipe away the memory, humiliation, and ill-feelings brought on by his dispute with Dani.

Whether Dani or anyone else forgave what had happened, Harvey sought to forgive himself. He hoped the swim would act as a baptism of sorts, a means of renewal, to learn from the past, move beyond mistakes, and start over. But, no matter what, Harvey continued to think himself as a fool for the "show" he put on at Buffalo Bills. It usually took time and even a few sleepless nights before he gave himself permission to get over major blunders ... real, imagined, or exaggerated.

Billy Joe found the exchange between Harvey and Dani to be comical. Harvey might see humor in words spoken out of anger and spite, later on. For now, he'd suffer from periods of self-loathing and torture.

Harvey and Billy Joe dried in their tent. Later, they dressed in hoody sweatshirts and shorts, then wandered to the Tanaka and Derry camp. Corky had spent the day under the care of Rodger, Ken, and Candi. The cantankerous dog somehow behaved himself around the children, except Rodney who remained separate from the others.

Harvey and Billy Joe engaged in a marshmallow and weenie roast with the family. It wasn't exactly the large campfire which warmed those surrounding it. There was a sense of community within a small group which bonded in love, trust, and friendship. Even then, there was an air of melancholy throughout the night. Early that next morning, the Tanakas and Derrys would pack up and return to The Dalles. Meanwhile, Harvey and Billy Joe had to retain their lives, responsibilities, and obligations in Grangeford. There were promises of trading e-mails, sending letters and postcards, the exchange of Christmas cards. They even discussed plans and hopes of reuniting at Fish Lake the following summer. No matter. Everyone harbored thoughts and fears that their goodbyes meant never seeing each other again. Laughter mixed with concealed tears.

Billy Joe fetched his guitar and banjo. Along with Barb, they belted out a series of cowboy, western, traditional songs and ballads as Streets of Laredo, Bury Me Not on the Lone Prairie, and Greensleeves. Privately, Billy Joe knew he wasn't the greatest singer in the world, and definitely needed improvement. In truth, Barb had him beat on a number of counts, despite being out of the music business for several years. Age had eroded her once beautiful voice. Neither Billy Joe nor Barb commented or made criticisms. Instead, they gave each other needed encouragement and words of kindness.

However, Barb granted Billy Joe some advice which, whether he liked it or not, remained with him for the rest of his life.

"I always heard that Nashville's a good town," she said. "But it's not always a nice place for budding pickers and singers. For everyone who makes a go of it, there are Heaven knows how many more who, after years of hard work and disappointment, turn tail and head on back home where they get unrewarding jobs, wondering and worrying and wishing on what mighta been had they just stuck it out a little longer."

Billy Joe said nothing. He sat there in the darkness, mulling over what Barb had just told him.

"You're a wonderful singer and a helluva guitar player," complimented Barb. "And you'll only get better. But give yourself time to get better, and learn. Learn from your mistakes, from trusting the wrong people, and taking the wrong turns or heading down dead-end streets. Your path will be filled with the wrong people and long days, months, and years heading down them dead-end streets."

Billy Joe frowned. His voice cracked and wavered as he voiced deep-seated concerns. "You make it sound like I'm gonna blow it."

"Oh, you're gonna fail, no need to worry about that. You're gonna have your failures, no matter what. What matters is your willingness and ability to get back up, brush yourself off, and keep on going."

"Don'tcha want me to make it?"

"I made the mistake of giving up. Oh sure, I had a good life. I have great kids and even better grandkids." Barb glanced at Angela and her two youngsters. "And I'm gonna have more good kids and grandkids. I've had a real good life. Truly blessed for it. I'd be lying if I said I don't fret, thinking if I coulda made a name for myself. No, Billy Joe. I don't want you to blow it." Barb's tone revealed disappointment and sadness. "I just don't want you to make the mistakes I made. If it means I gotta spend the next ten or twenty years in this wheelchair, I hope to one day turn on the radio and hear you giving your all doing songs you'll always be remembered for. It ain't gonna be easy. You're gonna get your ass kicked so hard you won't be able to sit down. But I hope you keep going and give it hell until you make a good living from it."

"Harvey's been to Nashville," said Billy Joe, anxiously. "But I ain't, yet. You think I oughta go there first thing, or? ... Or somewhere else?"

"In time, sure. But maybe not right away. Find yourself a decent audience in smaller towns before you set off for the big time. Play a few clubs in Seattle and Portland, learn, and fall on your butt where there ain't so many people to see you do it. Get back up, figure out how and where you went wrong, and try not to do it again. When you're ready, head off to Tulsa or Austin or Bakersfield, where some of the best got their starts before lighting out for Nashville. Get as good as you can, so when you get there you'll know better than to trust the worst people, and know ahead of time before you head down them dead end streets."

"Damn," breathed Billy Joe, on the brink of tossing his guitar into the campfire. "You make me wanna think twice about going into music, at all!"

"I ain't trying to hurt you, Billy Joe. I just don't want you to make the same mistakes I made and, believe me, I made them! I got screwed and screwed over in ways you can't never imagine! I hope and pray you find happiness and success. But it ain't gonna come easy. And it ain't always gonna be the ol' fashioned folk or country and western music you been strumming. Never know. Might find yourself being a back-up picker for someone, somewhere, playing music you don't like. But you'll do it if it means putting food on the table. It can be fun, but it sure ain't always fair or kind-hearted or honest. No matter what, I hope you never stop loving music. I never stopped loving it, even when I was raising a family or working some god-awful jobs to survive. I never stopped loving the music, and I sure hope you don't either."

Billy Joe pasted a nervous smile upon his face, nodded yes, and whispered, "Thanks!"

Barb cradled the banjo in her arms, and began singing a Cajun tune titled Jole Blon. She slapped Billy Joe's shoulder and called for him to play and sing along.

With a loud, rebel yell, Billy Joe let go of his worries and did what he was told.

***

Music, food, and conversation set a mood for the night. Everyone sat around the campfire and enjoyed what would never, and could never, be replaced or repeated. Everyone agreed that the evening was pure magic, moments destined to become warm memories. There were desires to bottle up the good times and replay them during periods of loneliness, or on long, dreary winter nights.

Sometime that evening, Angela led Harvey into her tent, where again she spoke in private.

Harvey and Angela sat together, in a darkened corner of the tent. Angela handed Harvey a bottle of regional wine, allowed him to take a drink, then took a sip. "The kids love you and Billy Joe," she spoke in a quiet, somber tone. "We could've just come up here and had a real boring time by the lake, but you two helped make it truly special."

"I love you, too," whispered Harvey. "You guys gave Billy Joe someone to show off to. As for me ..." He stopped. "I don't know how you found out about Billy Joe and me. I had no idea it was so ... Obvious. But, anyway. Thanks for being so cool about it."

"It's all good, Harvey. Life can only get better. I hope you and Billy Joe the very best!"

Harvey nodded his head and smiled.

"When do you think you'll tell your parents?" asked Angela, hesitantly.

A jolt of fear sprinted down Harvey's spine.

"I'm sorry!" apologized Angela. "I didn't mean to upset you!"

Harvey frowned, unable to mask his discomfort.

Angela sighed. "It's just that ... It only seems fair that they know about you two, sooner or later. Don't you agree?"

Harvey merely shrugged.

"Your folks sound kind of cool to me," said Angela. "The kind of folks I only wish I had growing up. Something tells me they'll be fine about it, once you tell them."

"But what if they're not?"

"Wouldn't it be easier for you to tell them, or risk having them find out by accident?"

Harvey said nothing. Angela had a point. But, getting the truth out to Terry and Elaine sounded easier than it would eventually be. Harvey dreaded the day he'd come out to his family. He owed his parents the truth, all right, but still feared their response.

Harvey didn't set out to be gay. He wondered why he was destined or doomed for such a fate. As before, he questioned if it was an act of God, Mother Nature, or an "error" of biology.

Harvey rested Angela's hand in his and asked, "You think we'll ever be able to get back together, again?"

Silence.

"I mean ..." Harvey took in a deep breath. "I know that, tomorrow, we gotta say our goodbyes, go our separate ways. But do you think?... You think we'll ever get a chance to hang out again, or even hear from each another?"

"Well, we can only hope, can we?" said Angela. She took another swig of wine, then handing the bottle to Harvey. "You and Billy Joe have been marvelous, and I'll always remember the great times we've had up here." Angela kissed Harvey on the cheek. "Promise me one thing ... please?"

"What's that?" sobbed Harvey.

"Promise me that you'll always be happy. That's all." Angela wiped away a tear, streaming from one eye. "Just ... Just be happy ..."

23

As the hour approached midnight, it was time to break up the festivities and go to bed. Billy Joe and Barb ended with Auld Lang Syne, as Angela and Harvey cleaned everything from around the tables, barbeque, and chairs. The two threw soiled paper cups and plates into the campfire, which by now was nearly extinguished for the exception of a few smoldering coals. Angela planned to stay awake and allow the fire to completely die down. At the moment, it was time for the youngsters to hit the sack and rest up for their trip home to The Dalles, early that next morning.

Billy Joe got to his feet, collected his guitar and banjo, and wished Barb a very pleasant sleep. "Ma'am," he spoke, tipping his cap with one hand and shaking Barb's hand with the other. "You got no idea how much it meant to me to jam with you these last couple of nights. If I live to be a hundred, I ain't gonna forget how much of a kick I got outa it. I for damn sure ain't gonna forget what you told me."

Barb graciously placed Billy Joe's hand in hers and gave it a tight squeeze. Despite her attempts to hold back the emotions, she tried yet failed to prevent a few tears from running down both cheeks. The few hours Barb spent with Billy Joe were a reminder of fleeting youth, when freedoms are taken for granted and responsibilities are few ... A time when she belonged to a troupe which could never hold onto a band name or maintain the services of a drummer ... A time when dreams of a career in music were shattered due to endless conflicts, along with the needs to support a family. "You're a fine young man," Barb complimented, her voice cracking. "And you're a helluva good singer and guitar player. You're likely to get yourself into a real tough business. But somehow ... Some way ... Something just tells me you're gonna do real well."

"Thanks," said Billy Joe. He was reluctant to call it a night, and wanted to perform old time songs and hymns with Barb for all eternity. It was not to be, and both of them knew it.

There was so much more Barb wished to share with Billy Joe, but the words somehow refused to come. The best she could do was give him a strained, crooked smile, as her eyes grew increasingly dampened and red.

"Don't you worry," responded Billy Joe, upholding teen cockiness and bravado as he staved off the painful realities of saying goodbye. "One of these days you're gonna turn on the radio and there I'll be, acting like a bigshot on the Grand Ol Opry."

Barb simply nodded 'yes" and left it at that.

Harvey experienced a dull, gnawing ache in the pit of his stomach. Although he managed a smile as he stepped toward Angela, the finality of speaking his farewells nearly got the better of him. He pasted on a brave face (as this is what a man's gotta do when a man's gotta do it ... Right?), and hoped never to become a blubbering idiot while saying goodbye. What he owed Angela was beyond evaluation. Confiding his deepest of secrets to her was a needed oasis in a world which was all-too-often intolerant and cruel.

"Try not to give your folks too hard of a time," Harvey said to Rodger and Ken, then shook their hands.

"Unless we can get away with it," commented Rodger, cleverly.

"Thanks," responded Ken, wearing a toothy grin as he threw his arms around Harvey in a bear hug. "You been way cool, man!"

Yeah, thanks for being our lifeguard," said Rodger, as he also embraced Harvey.

"It was fun," answered Harvey. "Have a safe trip home tomorrow."

"Goodnight," said Ken, as he and Rodger retreated into their tents.

"Goodnight," Harvey said back in a near-whisper. Slowly, he approached Candi who spent much of the evening kneeling by the fire with Corky at her side.

Lost in his own chaotic thoughts, Harvey reached down to shake Candi's hand. What Harvey didn't know was that Corky had taken a defensive attitude toward Candi, and attempted to bite his arm off.

Harvey swiftly pulled his hand back, as Corky got on all fours and stepped in his direction.

"Corky," scolded Billy Joe, pulling the angry dog away at the collar.

Harvey shook his head, in disgust. Meanwhile, Candi stood to give him a hug.

Once again, Corky let out a high-pitched howl and lunged at Harvey.

"Looks like I better get him outa here," said Billy Joe, cradling his guitar and banjo in one arm while holding Corky back with the other. He glanced toward Harvey and motioned toward their own camp. "Reckon we oughta mosey back on over?"

"In a minute," mumbled Harvey. "I'll be there in a bit."

Billy Joe smiled, tipped his hat toward Angela and Barb, then led Corky away.

Harvey wasn't the only one overwhelmed by sadness and despair over this parting of company. Angela, too, was hesitant in voicing an adios, but saw no way to avoid it. She had grown very fond of Harvey, and searched for the right words to express her feelings. The best she could come up with was, "Well, take care of yourself."

Harvey merely shrugged.

"Don't worry," assured Angela. "We might have time tomorrow to chat, before going home."

Harvey smiled. "That'd be great."

An awkward silence separated Harvey and Angela. Seconds felt more like minutes. The two wanted so much to say to each other, and had so little time in saying it.

"I wish you only the best," whispered Angela, resting one hand on Harvey's shoulders, "when it comes to ... You talking to your folks about ..."

Fear jolted through Harvey like lightning.

"I just don't know what more to tell you," Angela went on, hoping never to give Harvey reasons to be angry with her. "I know it's got to be hard, and I can't be there when the day comes for you to have that chat with them."

"Yeah," whispered Harvey." I know."

"All I can tell you is that I think ... I'm sure it's going to be all right."

Harvey rolled his eyes back and sighed. "I hope."

"Me too, Harvey," agreed Angela. "Me too."

With that, Harvey gave Angela a warm embrace. "I ... I can't thank you enough for your ... For all your understanding and support."

"You've been absolutely wonderful, Harvey!" said Angela. "I'm so glad we got a chance to meet. It's been so much fun having you and Billy Joe around."

"The same," breathed Harvey, slowly breaking away from Angela. He wasn't yet ready to leave, and wished he could say more. But the hour was late, and there would never be opportunity enough to say everything running through his mind. Yet, the shortest goodbyes were indeed the best. "See you tomorrow?" he requested, in a plea.

Angela smiled as she gripped Harvey's hands in hers. "As long as we're still here," she responded. "You're welcome in our campground any time you'd like to come by."

Harvey turned to follow Billy Joe. In the corner of one eye, he took notice of Rodney, still sitting alone in the same exact chair he resided in throughout his stay at Fish Lake. As always, Rodney was preoccupied with his music, along with the portable game he constantly played.

Harvey shot a quick glance at Angela, chuckled, then quietly stepped toward Rodney. "Good night, Rod," he said, wearing the most heartfelt of smiles. "Hope you sleep well tonight, and have a really awesome trip home tomorrow."

Rodney briefly looked up from his game to see Harvey standing next to him, hand extended in a gesture of camaraderie and friendship.

Rodney gave Harvey a lopsided smile, reached out to shake his hand ...

Then returned to his music and portable game as if nothing ever happened ...

24

As Harvey wandered back to the tent he shared with Billy Joe and Corky, he was moments away from something he especially looked forward to. Before starting their trip, he and Billy Joe had discussed making love outside, under the stars.

And on that very night, they'd see it through.

Months before, Harvey and Billy Joe had lost their virginity to each other in a dark, dusty, musty garage on the McBain property. It was hardly a romantic or joyous occasion. Their next sexual encounter was in Harvey's bedroom, while Terry and Elaine attended a Democratic Party fundraiser in the Tri-Cities. That experience was far more enjoyable, yet still came off as nerve-racking and hurried. The two boys were in constant fear of Terry and Elaine getting home early to catch them in the act.

But now, Harvey and Billy Joe yearned to find Paradise, surrounded by the beauties and splendor of the Wallowa Mountains in the moonlight.

Harvey and Billy Joe laid out an open sleeping bag behind their tent, where they'd be secluded. Harvey placed a feather pillow at one end of the sleeping bag, and prayed for a night that he'd cherish forever.

Harvey stepped into the tent. Corky was curled in one corner, and snarled at his arrival. Billy Joe wanted the dog to fall asleep. The only light came from a flashlight on his cellphone. Billy Joe scrounged around for the one piece of clothing he planned to wear while making love to Harvey.

Harvey peeled out of his hoody, then slipped on a white, long-sleeved tee-shirt with I LOVE OREGON scrawled upon the front. An image of a heart rested on a map of the state, where the city of Grangeford sat in the northeast.

"Aw!" cheered Billy Joe, retrieving a Grangeford High cap hidden among a clutter of coolers and backpacks. He sat the cap upon his head and turned it around, backwards. "Got it!"

Harvey giggled, nervously.

Billy Joe removed his shirt and cutoffs, and sat them next to an empty beer bottle. He took Harvey's hand and led him outside.

Harvey's heart raced as he followed Billy Joe to the sleeping bag, outside. Billy Joe's naked body revealed itself in the bright full moon.

Billy Joe sat on the sleeping bag and crossed his legs. Whether he was conscious of his nudity, he made no comment on it. Harvey thought too much of it. Cautiously, he glanced all around, making sure no one eavesdropped on them. It was eerily still and quiet, among silhouettes of trees and the surrounding mountain peaks. A cool, gentle breeze swept through the campground.

"Relax," urged Billy Joe, softly rubbing Harvey's face. "Make yourself at home. Nothin' to worry about."

Harvey took a deep breath and, mustering his courage, removed a pair of gym shorts and tossed them at the foot of the sleeping bag.

Seductively, Billy Joe tucked at Harvey's briefs, as if to ask *What about these?*

Harvey gave Billy Joe a sheepish grin and shrugged his shoulders.

"C'mon," urged Billy Joe, softly. "Please?"

Panic swept over Harvey. He wanted to have sex with Billy Joe, yet wondered if this was the time or place for it. Still, it was something the two had long discussed, and there was no evading it ... was there?

"Please?" repeated Billy Joe, this time as a command.

Harvey cautiously slipped out of his drawers and exposed himself to one he treasured more than anyone else on Earth. Hoping for a laugh, he carelessly threw his underwear, somewhere, in the darkness.

Harvey scooted next to Billy Joe, wearing only his long-sleeved tee. Any inhibitions he had gave way to freedom and liberation. Billy Joe placed one arm around Harvey, and kissed him on the lips. "I love you," he spoke. Oddly, his voice revealed sadness and regret.

Harvey sensed Billy Joe's despair, but said nothing.

"I ... I sometimes wonder ..." Billy Joe mumbled " ... and sometimes doubt ... if I ... if I'm good enough to make it in music."

"How come?" questioned Harvey.

"Well, shit, my picking and singing really sucked tonight! Couldn't ya tell?"

Although Billy Joe had room for improvement, he had gotten better ... Way better, than he was years before in middle school chorus. Eventually, he'd gain strength and maturity as an artist. He still had so much to learn, and much more to obtain.

"What makes you say that?" asked Harvey, resting his head upon Billy Joe's shoulder.

"I really wanted to nail it tonight. I tried, Harve. Goddamn it, I really tried! Think I only succeeded at sounding stupid!"

"No, you didn't!" laughed Harvey. "Everyone really got into it. They smiled and clapped and even sang along ... When they knew the words. You and Barb got everybody in an awesome mood. You turned what could've been a boring camping trip into a celebration!"

"I know, but ..." Billy Joe sighed. "I always wanted to yodel like Eddy Arnold in 'Cattle Call' and Slim Whitman or Jimmie Rodgers in pretty much everything they done! Goddamn it! Whenever I'm alone in my room, I sing along with them old songs, hoping to do right by 'em and all, do what all them dead guys had done. I'm blowing it, 'cause I can't god-damn yodel! I just can't! Had I been able to, I woulda showed just how good I am, and just how good I'll be when I ... when we get to Nashville." Billy Joe frowned. "If we ever get to Nashville. Now I'm wondering if may-be I ought not go to Nashville at all! I just don't think I'm good enough. All I'm gonna do is make myself sound stupid, like I did tonight."

"You didn't sound stupid. You did okay."

"'Okay'? Just 'okay'?"

"No! I didn't ..." Harvey rolled his eyes back and sighed. "You did bet-ter than 'okay'. Okay? Look, everyone had a great time, and so did I! You won them over, and ... Who knows? You might just do the same when you get to Nashville." Harvey grinned. "When we get to Nashville."

Billy Joe shrugged.

Harvey kissed Billy Joe's neck, below his right ear. "I'd rather go with you to Nashville, New York, or Hell on Earth, and see you try and fail, and hate yourself for not making a go of it."

"Ya think?"

"Do you want me to do well with my writing?" said Harvey.

"Hell, yeah! You're a helluva good writer, and I'll kill you if you don't work your ass off and get yourself noticed out there! If you only knew how much I love and respect and admire ... I love you, Harve, and I want you to be happy too!"

"That's exactly how I feel about you." Harvey cleared his throat. "Look, if you really want to yodel, then maybe ..." He hesitated. "Maybe tonight I can help you."

With that, Harvey laid flat upon the sleeping bag. Wearing only his 'I Love Oregon' tee-shirt and an eager grin, he spread his legs and invited Billy Joe to his body. "Mount up," he urged, his voice quivering in anxiety and anticipation. "Mount up and ride 'em, cowboy!"

***

"I love you," breathed Harvey, after what proved to be the most exciting, exhilarating, exhausting, and erotic adventure he ever had with Billy Joe McBain. "I love you so much!"

"I love you, too." Billy Joe showered Harvey with kisses. "I love ya more'n anything!"

Harvey placed his head to Billy Joe's chest. "I'm so lucky to have you in my life. I sometimes wonder why I deserve you."

Billy Joe ran his fingers along the seams of Harvey's shirt, then softly caressed his bare bottom. A slight wind swept across the boys' nude bodies. Billy Joe acted as security blanket over the most important person in his life. He considered fetching a quilt, or leading Harvey into the tent. For the moment, it was enough to stare into the endless night sky. "Harve?"

"Yeah?" asked Harvey.

"Thanks for what you said about my music."

"I meant it. I think you're really good! And really handsome." Harvey rubbed Billy Joe's upper lip. "I only wish you'd get rid of ... That."

"Why does everyone hate my mustache so much?"

"It's not a mustache. You just think it's a mustache."

"That's what Grandma Abigail says!"

"I like you better without it," admitted Harvey.

"Says the man who can't grow any whiskers at all." Billy Joe paused. "Harve?"

"Hmm?"

"Will you ..." Billy Joe took a deep breath, and released it in a sigh. "Marry me?"

Harvey gasped.

"I mean ..." Billy Joe laughed. "I mean ... not now. Not yet. I meant ... ya know, after we're out of high school. When we're paddling our own canoes, making our own calls, paying our own way."

"But aren't you still thinking about? ... The Army?"

Billy Joe groaned. "Well, I wanna serve our country. What's wrong with that? I always figured it was honorable to ..."

"But what if we get into another idiotic war?"

"I dunno about you. Jesus, Harve! You and your family's wussy-assed politics."

Harvey glared at Billy Joe.

Billy Joe grinned, nervously. "Sorry, I didn't mean 'wussy'."

"Then what did you mean?" demanded Harvey.

Billy Joe eyed a faint beam of light in the sky, which was the planet Jupiter. "Look. I know you guys hate war. I don't wanna join the Army because I like killing. I wanna keep the peace. I also hope ..." Billy Joe shrugged. "I'm also hoping that having a military background will help me when I ... when we get to Nashville. You know. Country music folks like knowing that the guy on stage did the right thing by giving a few years to the good ol' U S of A."

"What do you think they'll say once they find out you're married to me?"

Billy Joe hugged Harvey as tight as he could. "I don't give a hoot or a holler what others think. My grandparents are cool about it, and I know your folks will be too if you ever get the balls to tell them."

A jolt of fear sprinted through Harvey.

"People are gonna have to accept me ... Us ... as we really are," stated Billy Joe. "I ain't gonna flaunt the idea of me being a bisexual country singer, or you being a gay writer. But I ain't gonna hide it neither. I need you with me."

"I need you, too," agreed Harvey, on the verge of weeping. "You know what? When we were going at it, you want to know what I saw?"

"What?"

"There was a buck staring at us the whole time!" giggled Harvey. "Wonder if he knew what we were doing."

"Might be he got off on it!" snickered Billy Joe.

Harvey sucked in a deep breath. "It's weird. I kept thinking someone was watching us, when ... when we were doing it. And there he was, watching us the whole time!"

For a minute or two, Harvey and Billy Joe rarely spoke a word. They simply relaxed upon the sleeping bag, holding onto each other.

"You getting cold?" yawned Billy Joe.

"Kind of. You?"

"Yeah. Wanna go inside, or stay out here?"

"Stay out here."

Billy Joe wandered into the tent. Moments later, he returned with a thick quilt. He draped it over Harvey, then crawled inside. "G'night, Harve," he yawned. "Sleep well."

"You too," spoke Harvey, giving Billy Joe a goodnight kiss. "See you in the morning."

As Billy Joe quietly sang Beautiful Dreamer, Harvey stretched his tired body, closed his eyes, and gradually fell asleep.

25

Harvey woke to a bright, blazing sun hitting him in the eyes. He turned to one side, uncertain of where he was or how he even got there. He blinked once or twice, then wiped his sweaty face.

Harvey soon realized he'd been sleeping outside, high in the Wallowa Mountains. He peeled out from under the quilt, blinked his eyes, and took a moment to gain his bearings.

To his shock and horror, Harvey also remembered that he was dressed only in a long-sleeved tee-shirt with the words 'I Love Oregon' ... and nude from the waist down!

Harvey got to his knees, searching frantically for the gym shorts and underwear which he carelessly discarded in the night. Panic engulfed him. He hoped no one saw him as he looked everywhere for his missing clothing.

Harvey desperately scrounged through his bedding. He finally located his gym shorts near the edge of the sleeping bag. His underwear dangled from a nearby bush. He hastily slipped into the drawers and shorts, then hopped to his feet. He glanced at the cell phone which were in the pockets of his shorts. It was nearly eight in the morning.

Harvey turned toward the campsite where the Tanakas and Derrys were camped over the past few days. It was now empty. The only signs that the family had been there were a few dead coals left in a firepit, long extinguished.

Harvey slouched. He really wanted to spend more time with that bunch, and grew sad because it was not to be. He felt safe and accepted with them ... Most especially Angela. The woman remained a true friend, supporter, and an ally. Harvey hoped to have an opportunity to chat with Angela, and further enjoy her companionship, warm words, and smile. He begged to further confide with Angela, and even speak of last night's lovemaking to Billy Joe.

Sadness overwhelmed Harvey. He feared never seeing that family ever again, people he had known so briefly yet cared about so dearly. Emptiness, disappointment, and feelings of loss took charge.

He reminded himself that the last three letters of the word 'friend' always spelled "end".

Harvey recalled a trip he made with his mother Elaine across country on Greyhound. For three days, Harvey and Elaine were confined to a number of busses until they reached their destination of Washington DC. During that time, they had managed to obtain and develop companionship throughout the long commute. Harvey thought back to those he spent time and even broke bread with. He contemplated their names and faces, who they were and what they were. He knew about their lives, and reasons for traveling. He grew to value and appreciate their comradeship, born out of convenience and coincidence. And yet, neither he or Elaine had further contact with anyone spent on those miles toward the nation's capital, or those he encountered during the journey home. He remembered these folks' names and faces, and understood the joys and comforts he gained by their simply "being there". Yet, in the end there was nothing more, once those people departed carriers for the last time and went their separate ways ...

Never to be seen by Harvey or Elaine again.

And that's the way it goes ... doesn't it? Such are the pleasures, the pains, the rewards and dangers of being human. Nothing is just or fair. The journey of life is never as long as we'd like, and no one knows who or what they'll encounter. People gain hope, wisdom, truth. Too often it clearly renders ... nothing.

Absolutely nothing.

"They left a few minutes after six," explained Billy Joe, stepping from the tent. "Packed up before sunrise, and headed down the road. Said they wanted to be in The Dalles before noon."

"Why didn't you wake me?" whined Harvey.

"They didn't want me to." Billy Joe knew that Harvey's feelings were hurt. "You was asleep. They didn't wanna bother waking you up, and neither did I. They told me that as soon as I … as we get to Nashville, let 'em know so they'll be looking for my first album."

To Harvey's sudden delight and pleasure, there was a noticeable change in Billy Joe's appearance. "You shaved it off!" he cheered. "You shaved your mustache off!"

"Aw, well," commented Billy Joe, as if to say No big deal.

"You do that for me?" asked Harvey, lightly running one finger along Billy Joe's upper lip.

"You? Naw," claimed Billy Joe, though his expressions said otherwise. "I got where I was tasting food three hours after I ate it. Ya like me better without it?"

Harvey grinned in approval. "A lot better. Honestly, I never liked that caterpillar. I'm glad it's finally gone. Please don't grow it back."

"Aw, ya never know." Billy Joe and Harvey entered the tent. Corky responded with a growl. "Might try a goatee next time."

Harvey rolled his eyes back and sighed.

"We better head out too," informed Billy Joe. "Let's pack everything up, throw it in the back of the rig. We'll chow down at Main Street Cafe, since you wore out our welcome at Buffalo Bills yesterday."

Harvey groaned.

"You can't help it," taunted Billy Joe. "Everything offends you liberals, don't it? One wrong word, and the shit hits the fan."

"Har-de-har-har," responded Harvey, fetching the cooler which had been filled with beer and ice. By now, the ice had melted to stale water, while a few beers floated to the surface. Harvey went outside and carefully dumped the water to one side, while preventing the full bottles from spilling onto the ground. He closed the lid, jumped into the back of the GMC, and rested the cooler near the cab.

By now, Billy Joe had his hands filled with fishing tackle, which he never once used during their vacation. He hoped to do a bit of fishing, but never got around to it. Despite that, he regarded the three days away from Grangeford as a success. It was best to remember the vacation for what it was, not what it might have been.

Harvey contemplated his love for Billy Joe … His Prince Charming, his Rhett Butler, his one and only Knight in Shining Armor. Billy Joe was not perfect. Then again, who was? Harvey was far from perfect! Still, he was blessed to have Billy Joe in his life.

Harvey wondered if he and Billy Joe had time for a "quickie", before taking down the tent and leaving. Without warning, he gave Billy Joe a passionate kiss on the lips.

Corky leaped to his feet and bit into Harvey's right hand.

Harvey screamed as he pulled away from Billy Joe. He shot a swift glance at his injured hand. Corky had drawn blood.

That wasn't the end of it. Corky decided to finish the job by lunging at Harvey's face.

Harvey kicked, slugged, slapped, and cursed Corky, fearing for his life while struggling to halt the crazed and jealous dog. Out of desperation, he latched onto a long, heavy black flashlight from the ground, and whacked it across Corky's forehead.

Corky let out a shriek, then fled from the tent with his tail between his legs.

"Harve!" shouted Billy Joe. "Just what the? ..."

Billy Joe's protests were cut short by the sounds of screeching tires, a loud, dull thud! Corky's high-pitched yelps, and Harvey dropping the flashlight at his feet.

Billy Joe dashed outside, with Harvey in pursuit.

What Billy Joe saw next haunted him for the rest of his life. Corky lay in front of a bright silver, Subaru station wagon. The dog shook and convulsed involuntarily, as blood shot from his nose and mouth.

Inside the station wagon was a balding man with a receding mustache, sitting next to a homely, middle-aged woman who spouted a string of profanities at him. The hapless fellow had already been put through a wringer since leaving Bend the day before. In the back seat was a trio of small, freckled-faced children, ages five to nine, mortified by the knowledge that their dad had just struck and killed Corky.

Billy Joe released a mournful cry. Meanwhile, Harvey stood quietly back. His thoughts were divided between Billy Joe's devastating loss, and the joys in realizing that Corky was no more.

Billy Joe knelt to Corky who remained upon the gravel driveway, his eyes glazing over in an inescapable stare of death. "Corky!" he shrieked, holding onto the dog's limp body. At first, his mind refused to believe what had just taken place. Gradually, the cruel, painful truth swept through his consciousness.

Billy Joe wouldn't miss Corky right away. In time, he'd suffer the loss when he'd no longer have the hound at his feet, a constant friend during long winter nights in his bedroom.

The Subaru's driver got out of the car, wearing a look of confusion, disbelief, and regret. "He ... Is he okay?"

"Hell no, he ain't okay!" bawled Billy Joe, getting to his feet with Corky cradled in both arms. "Can'tcha see he ain't okay, ya dumb son of a bitch?"

The driver stared at the pathetic sight of Billy Joe and Corky. He barely registered Billy Joe's insult against him.

"I'm sorry the dog ran in front of you," said Harvey, his voice lacking sincerity. In truth, he felt worse for the Subaru's driver than he ever would for Corky. He stepped forward, hoping to make amends for Billy Joe's verbal assault.

"Well, if my shit-for-brains husband had been watching where the hell he was going," the driver's wife screeched, in a nasally voice, "then the shit-for-brains dog wouldn't o' been hit in the first place!"

For a few awkward seconds, silence separated everyone. Finally, Billy Joe disappeared behind the tent, with Corky.

"Sorry for what happened," repeated Harvey, blankly.

"Not near as sorry as I am," the driver mumbled. "Is there? ... Anything I can do?"

"It wasn't your fault," said Harvey, failing to mention what he did to Corky in defending himself. "Things happen, and ... Well, things happen."

The driver reached into his wallet for a wad of paper money. He shoved the money in the palm of Harvey's hand which still dripped blood from Corky's attack.

Harvey shook his head. "Look, mister, you don't gotta ..."

"Yeah, I do," the driver argued. "I gotta. Take it. Please, just take it."

Harvey pasted on a strained smile. "Really, mister. You don't have to pay us for a thing."

"Take it before my wife uses it to cover a bar tab or a session with her queer hair stylist!" the driver shouted. He got back into the car, turned the ignition over, and drove toward the campsite which the Tanakas and Derrys had left just hours before.

Harvey watched the Subaru peel away. From a distance, he heard one of the kids shrieking as the wife cursed out her ever-suffering husband. The only thing remaining from the accident was a small puddle of blood, dissipating into the loose soil and gravel of the driveway.

Harvey shoved the money into one pocket of his gym shorts, then stepped behind the tent where Billy Joe wrapped Corky into the sleeping bag. "Wait a minute!" he called out. "What do you think you're doing?"

"Hell does it look like I'm doing?" screamed Billy Joe.

"But ..." Harvey rolled his eyes back and sighed. "Isn't that where we ..."

"Screwed last night?" interrupted Billy Joe. "Well, what of it?"

Harvey frowned.

"It's just pieces of cloth, not a goddamn shrine!" argued Billy Joe. "Okay, so we did the nasty on it. What the hell? You wanna hang it up on your wall, keep it for all-times-sake, show it off to all our friends? Why should I care if it's where I humped you? Well, for right now, it just happens to be the shroud that I'm gonna bury my dog in! Got anything else you wanna say about it?"

"I'm sorry about Corky," Harvey whimpered.

Billy Joe said nothing. He continued tearing down what remained of the camp. Occasionally, he gave Harvey spiteful stares, as if to blame him for the demise of a mean-spirited and jealous dog.

26

The trip from Fish Lake to Halfway was tense. It was strange not having Corky sharing the cab with Harvey and Billy Joe, vigilantly guarding his master. Billy Joe's behavior didn't help matters. He refused to speak, even after Harvey repeatedly uttered, "Sorry about Corky," or "Sorry about your dog," or just, "Sorry."

Nothing eased Billy Joe's caustic emotions. If anything, Harvey's attempts to comfort him only made his driving more reckless and unpredictable. Billy Joe only answered with comments such as "Whatever," or "Who the hell cares?"

Constantly, Harvey urged Billy Joe to slow down around narrow, hairpinned corners, on passes with loose gravel and little traction, or along hillsides which meant certain death should the GMC leave the road.

Eventually, Harvey glared at Billy Joe and asked, "What's your problem now? You missing Corky so much you want to join him in the Hereafter?"

After what proved to be a perilous and frightening journey, the GMC entered Halfway. Billy Joe stopped in front of the Main Street Café, a structure which was more than a century old. The café's second story was used as a hotel and office space. The café and tavern had recently been remodeled, which breathed new life into the aging building.

As Harvey went inside, Billy Joe made sure that Corky remained concealed within the sleeping bag.

Harvey found a comfortable table and awaited Billy Joe's arrival. An attractive, young female server gave him a couple of menus, silverware, and glasses of water.

Moments later, Billy Joe entered the diner. He was still not up to talking. He ignored the servers and other customers. This, even after several patrons recognized him from the charity event, and complimented his marksmanship.

Harvey requested two scrambled eggs and hash browns with gravy. Billy Joe simply asked for toast. He hardly touched his meal, even after it was brought to him.

Harvey repeatedly stated how badly he felt for Corky. At one point, he even handed Billy Joe the money that the Subaru driver gave him. The money added up to a hundred dollars in fives, tens, and twenties.

"Why didn't you just tell that bastard to shove it up his ass?" snapped Billy Joe.

Harvey rolled his eyes back and sighed.

"And just what the hell gave you the right to hit Corky with that goddamn flashlight?" snapped Billy Joe.

"He bit me!" Harvey revealed the teeth marks on his injured hand. "What else was I supposed to do? Your asshole dog attacked me when I kissed ..." Harvey realized that his voice was carrying, and quickly lowered it. "Did you expect me just to stand there and let him fly into the middle of me? I thought he was gonna kill me! I had to do something!"

"Corky's dead because of you!"

"Because of me? Don't you care about what he did to me? Or did you love?" Harvey stopped, conscious of those near him. "Did you care more about Corky than you do for me?"

"Corky was my dog, Harve! He was my dog since he was born, five years ago! He was my dog long before you was my boyfriend! Doesn't that mean a damned thing to you?"

Harvey reached into his wallet for enough cash to cover his breakfast, along with a tip. "Screw this," he mumbled. "I've had enough of your bullshit. I ... I'm just gonna go outside and wait for you to stop feeling sorry for yourself!"

With that, Harvey stepped outside and began crossing the street to the GMC.

Harvey spotted Dani wandering toward him, from a nearby location known as Pat's Park. It was a shaded area covered with grass, featuring an outdoor stage where musical and dramatic performances were held during the summer and early fall.

With Dani was a young man, around seventeen or eighteen. The young man was well over six feet tall, with a military-style buzz-cut and sinewy physique. He carried himself with confidence and authority, which bordered on conceit.

"Where do you think you're going?" questioned Dani, once she and the young man intercepted Harvey. "I got something I wanna say to you!"

Harvey considered on fleeing into the GMC's cab, where he'd roll up the windows and lock the doors. What good would that do? The temperature outside was already warm. It got even hotter in the cab, with both windows sealed shut. Harvey had no idea what Dani or the young man had in mind. Obviously, this was no social call.

"Answer me when I'm talking to you!" screamed Dani. "Where's your butt-buddy? Where's your darling Billy Joe Bad-Ass McBain?" Dani smiled, wickedly. "You're all alone, now."

Harvey was petrified, but didn't want Dani or the young man knowing it. His frightened expression gave him away. No matter. He had to do something ... anything ... to prevent what Dani and the young man had in mind. Perhaps this was the time to apologize and make an amends for what he said to her the day before. He was more than willing to swallow his pride, if it avoided taking a beating. "Look, if you're still upset over our argument yesterday," he said, his voice high-pitched and jittery. "Then I'm sorry ... I'm sorry, okay? Okay? Look, I'm sorry! If ... is it enough to say that maybe I was wrong? And ... maybe ... we might even become friends?"

"Why would I want to be friends with the likes of you?" Dani shoved Harvey against the GMC's fender. "I don't make friends with homos, and I'm not about to be your friend after what you said to me yesterday!"

Harvey's heart skipped a beat. He didn't know what Dani had found out about his relationship with Billy Joe (unless Debra spilled the beans ... The mouthy little owl!). "What?" he stuttered. "What? ... What makes you think I'm?"

"Uh ... uh ... uh ... uh!" giggled Dani, closing both eyes as she placed one hand over her crotch. "I love you, Billy Joe! I love you, so ... Oh! ... Uh ... uh ... uh ... UH!"

Harvey's face revealed anger and unbridled fear.

"I saw what you and Billy Joe did last night!" laughed Dani. "You had no idea we watched it the whole time, did you? Did you?"

The air rushed out of Harvey's lungs and mouth. Panic took control now.

"We caught Billy Joe pumping on you from behind!" laughed Dani. "'Uh ... uh ... uh! Oh, I love you, Billy! I love you so very ... Uh ... uh ... uh ...'"

Without giving it a single thought, Harvey slugged Dani right into the nose and mouth. Dani flew backwards, with blood shooting from both nostrils. She lost her balance and landed, butt-first, onto the sidewalk.

The young man lifted Harvey by his neck, a foot or more off the ground, then shook him like a helpless rag doll.

Harvey struggled to break free by slapping, kicking, and flailing at the young man. Oxygen was cut off from his throat and lungs. His face altered to a bright red as he battled to gain a breath which never came. Harvey opened his mouth in a mute plea. Saliva dripped from both corners of his mouth. His eyes bulged wildly from their sockets.

Slowly, gradually, painfully, Harvey began to lose consciousness.

The young man then dropped him to the curb.

Harvey crumbled onto the concrete, where he was lodged between the sidewalk and GMC. He gasped desperately for needed air, as tears spilled from his eyes.

In the distance, he heard the faint sounds of the Main Street Cafe's doors swing open, then shut. A familiar voice sang, "Oh, I'm a good ol' rebel, now that's just what I am'", as footsteps approached the GMC.

The young man grabbed Harvey by his arm and lifted him to his feet. Harvey attempted to remain standing. He felt dizzy, disoriented, and wobbly.

Dani slowly got to her feet. Blood caked her lips and chin. Dani was about to send a clenched fist into Harvey's gut, then took notice of Billy Joe coming toward her. "Well, if it ain't Billy Joe McBain!" she screeched, mockingly. "But you can call him ... 'Brokeback Mountain'!"

A sly chuckle slipped from the young man's mouth.

"Come to your little Harvey-boy's rescue?" growled Dani. "You pathetic, cowboy queer!"

"Do something, Billy Joe!" Harvey begged in a raspy voice, fighting to catch his breath. "Do something!"

"'Billy Joe'?" the young man asked, in a cocky voice. "That what you call yourself? 'Billy Joe'?"

"That's the name my mom gave me when I was born," responded Billy

Joe, undaunted. "That's what's on my birth certificate, my Social Security card, hunter safety, driver's license, my Bi-Mart Membership ..."

"Sounds like a fag's name to me," the young man snickered.

"Well maybe ... Maybe not," said Billy Joe. "But you wanna know what they call me up at the Umatilla Reservation?"

"What's that?" the young man questioned. "'Screams Like a Bitch'?"

"Nope." Billy Joe shook his head, with a self-assured grin. "Not even close. Why, on the rez, them folks refer to me as ... Billy Jack."

Harvey rolled his eyes back and sighed.

"Dani," Billy Joe said, rubbing his forehead in disgust as he paraphrased a line from the film 'Billy Jack'. "I want you to know that I try ... I really try. When all of our friends at school tell me to control my temper and be as passive and non-violent like they are. I try ... I really try." Billy Joe turned his attention upon Harvey. "But when I see ... This boy of such a beautiful spirit, who is so special to me. And I think of the number of years he's going to have to carry this in his memory ..."

"Billy Joe ..." whispered Harvey, begging him to stop.

" ... The savagery of this idiotic moment of yours." Billy Joe gritted his teeth. "I just go berserk ..."

With that, Billy Joe belted Dani across the face, and once again sent her to the pavement.

Profanities and threats slipped from Dani's mouth, as she curled up in a ball and wept.

The young man knelt down to check on Dani. "You? ... Are you all right?" he asked, in shock and sympathy.

"Hell no, I'm not all right!" screamed Dani. "What does it look like, y' moron?"

A few patrons stepped out of the café. Their attention glued to the drama playing out across the street.

Billy Joe opened the passenger-side door, then carefully sat Harvey upon the seat. "You okay?" he asked, running his fingers through Harvey's long, blonde hair.

"Not really," breathed Harvey.

"Don't just stand there with your thumb up your ass!" Dani screamed at the young man. "Kill the son of a bitch!"

The young man stepped toward Billy Joe. He was considerably taller than his opponent, and outweighed him by fifty pounds or more. Even then, he couldn't mask his fear.

Billy Joe looked the young man squarely in the eyes, with a mischievous smile.

"You ... You're pretty good at hit-hit-hitting g-girls ... ain'tcha?" the young man stuttered. "You ...you think you can give me the same treatment, you ... You ... You half-breed c- c- coward?"

"Don't look like I got a choice now, does it," responded Billy Joe, maintaining a calm facade. "You know what I think I'm gonna do then, just for the hell of it? I'm gonna take this right foot, and I'm gonna wop you on that side of the face. And you wanna know something? There ain't a damned thing you're gonna be able to do about it."

Billy Joe tried, yet failed, to slam one foot into the young man's jaw. This left him off-balance and vulnerable ... A situation which the young man swiftly took advantage of.

The young man grabbed Billy Joe's elevated foot, and lifted it skyward. This sent Billy Joe spinning wildly in the air, then descent headfirst toward the street.

A split-second later, Billy Joe slammed against the dust, dirt, and black top with a crushing thud!

Billy Joe saw lightning bolts and stars. Excruciating pain jolted from his skull, and exploded down the spine. He lay motionless near the front right tire of the GMC. Blood drained from his swelling face and forehead.

"Billy Joe!" shrieked Harvey. His pleas voiced an undying love for his own private Prince Charming, battered and bruised upon Main Street. He took Billy Joe's hand, then rested him against the GMC's bumper. "Answer me!" he cried. "Answer me, damn you! Please answer me!"

Billy Joe snickered at his own expense.

Once Dani picked herself from the sidewalk, she made a feeble kick at Billy Joe, but nailed Harvey by accident. Blinded by extreme rage and fury, she sent one foot into Billy Joe's torso.

It wasn't Harvey or Billy Joe to halt Dani's assault, but rather the young man with her. "Stop it!" the young man shouted, shoving Dani into a nearby picket fence.

"Like hell you say!" argued Dani. "Gimme a chance and I'll!"

"I told you to stop it!" the young man repeated. "Now, stop it!"

A number of patrons sprinted from the cafe, to the GMC. This included the server who had taken Harvey and Billy Joe's order, a ranch owner, his scrawny cowhand, and two high school boys. Most everyone had recognized Billy Joe and Dani from the charity competition. They admired Billy

Joe for his marksmanship, and immediately took his side in this skirmish.

The two high school boys picked Billy Joe up off the street.

Billy Joe slowly regained his bearings. He glanced at the two high schoolers, forced a grin upon his face, and mumbled, "'Which way did he go, George? Which way did he go?'"

The server dashed back to the diner, and soon returned with a damp rag and paper towels. She placed the rag to Billy Joe's head, then carefully wiped blood away from his face and hair.

"What about me?" complained Dani.

"What about you?" one of the high schoolers questioned, a blonde lad wearing a University of Oregon tee-shirt and baggy shorts.

"He ain't the only one who got hurt!" protested Dani.

"You're gonna get hurt a lot worse if you and the caveman don't leave!" the other high schooler answered. He wore a plaid shirt, jeans, and work boots. He looked the part of a future farmer or rancher. His tanned skin and rough-hewn features told of someone who valued sweat and toil upon the land.

"Faggots!" screeched Dani. "You're nothing but a bunch of faggots!"

The two high schoolers glared at Dani.

Dani pointed at Harvey and Billy Joe. "You gotta be faggots to stick up for those two."

"'Faggots'?" the boy in the green shirt questioned.

"What makes you say that?" the ranch owner asked, an older gentleman with piercing eyes, a thick grey mustache, and a silver felt cowboy hat.

"We caught them screwing each other last night, at Fish Lake," informed Dani. "Had you been there you woulda saw it, too!"

"What makes you think I'd wanna see that?" the ranch owner commented. "Maybe you like to watch that crap, but not me. Sounds to me like you're the one who's got problems. I don't give a hoot or a holler if them fellas are that a-way." The ranch owner placed one hand on Billy Joe's shoulder. "Anybody who shoots as straight as this fella, why, he's a'right by me."

Dani stared at the ranch owner, on the verge of issuing an insult. Onlookers would have none of it. Their stern, angry expressions spoke more than words could say.

"Do yourself and everyone else a big favor and get the hell out of here," the ranch owner told the young man and Dani, like one accustomed to giving orders. "Go on, get outa here. Right now, before I compel you to do so."

Dani was about to tell the crowd to do something which was physically impossible. The young man shook his head and begged her not to. Hastily, he took Dani by the arm and led her toward the corner of Main and Record Street.

Dani resented being told off by those who she believed were below her. Once her and the young man got to a structure known as the Three-Color Building, she gave the citizens of Halfway words to remember her by. "Why don't you and the rest of you bastards eat shit and die?" she screamed, as loud as she could.

"Dani ..." the young man warned.

"You heard me!" Dani continued, her voice echoing throughout the streets. "Why don't you and everybody else in this shitty little town go screw yourselves? You and everyone else in this miserable, piece of shit town! Go eat shit and ... and ... and die!"

Seconds later, the young man led Dani to a dark red, Ford Mustang, parked in front of the post office. Once the two got in, the Mustang sped past the US Bank, on its way out of town.

"That crazy bitch can start fights in an empty room," commented Billy Joe.

"What makes ya say that?" the high schooler in the U of O shirt asked.

Harvey frowned. "She's from Elgin."

"That explains it then," the ranch owner snickered. "Knew there had to be something wrong with her."

The ranch owner wished Harvey and Billy Joe the best of luck, then wandered back into the diner. There, he hoped to finish his pastry, sip a cup of hot coffee, and continue arguing with other landowners over local politics.

The two high schoolers walked Harvey and Billy Joe to a wooden bench outside of the diner. Meanwhile, the server fetched another damp cloth.

"Tony Bennett mighta left his heart in San Francisco," Billy Joe grunted, as he rested upon the bench. "Think I left my brains splattered across the street."

Dale and Janice Endicott quickly stepped outside of the diner. They were the married couple who had benefitted from the charity competition. They were about to compliment Billy Joe for his shooting skills. However, the sight of blood trickling from Billy Joe's face and forehead was shocking and alarming.

"Get the first aid kit," Janice ordered Dale, welcoming herself to the bench next to Harvey and Billy Joe. She softly rested Billy Joe's hand in hers, and upheld a stoic expression to conceal a maternal concern.

"Aw, hell, I'm awright," claimed Billy Joe, in embarrassment and anger.

"I'm not so sure," mumbled Janice, carefully examining Billy Joe's injured head. "You think I better call you an ambulance?"

"Why do you wanna 'call me an ambulance'?" giggled Billy Joe, in a lame attempt at humor. "I ain't no ambulance!"

Harvey rolled his eyes back and sighed.

Janice didn't know whether to laugh at Billy Joe's humor, or slap his face off. "All right then, smartass," she responded, in frustration. "Do you think I'd better get you an ambulance?"

"That's the last thing you oughta do," said Billy Joe.

"Janice might be right," told Harvey, nervously. "For all we know, you might have cracked your skull open."

"You know me better'n that, Harve!" cackled Billy Joe. "I did more damage to the asphalt than it did to me. I'm too Mick, too Spic, too Injun to feel any pain. Ain't nothing in my head to damage. Ain't nothing up there but tree bark and rocks."

Dale returned from an aging Dodge Ram, carrying a brown leather pouch with first aid supplies along with a bottle of Jim Beam.

Janice reached into the kit and went to work on Billy Joe. Despite Billy Joe's objections, she was determined to assist him. Janice cleansed the wounds, then dabbed gauze into a foul-smelling liquid which stung like sin. Billy Joe released a loud squall once it was applied to his head.

Dale chuckled as he allowed Billy Joe to take a swig of whiskey . The liquor was fiery and bitter, and burned all the way down. "If one thing don't fix you up," said Dale, with a hearty grin, "the other one will."

Billy Joe snickered.

"That was some mighty good shooting yesterday," complimented Dale, slapping Billy Joe's back. "Thought you mighta had old Cliff beat. I sure was rooting for ya."

"Thanks," whispered Billy Joe, as Janice bandaged his face and forehead.

"But if I didn't know no better, I swear you let Cliff whip ya," stated

Dale. "Now, c'mon kid, you can tell me. You didn't let him whip ya? Did ya?"

"What gave you that idea?" questioned Billy Joe, glaring at Harvey.

Harvey blushed, lowered his head, but said nothing.

"Well, if ya don't mind," said Dale. "I'd be right pleased to pay for you fellas' breakfasts, soon as the wife gets done torturing ya."

Harvey and Billy Joe smiled eagerly and happily accepted the offer.

27

Once they finished breakfast, Harvey and Billy Joe returned to the GMC. It was late in the morning. There were desires in getting home, to hot showers and clean clothes. Pressing to Billy Joe were needs to get Corky in the ground. He now suffered painful realizations that he'd have long, difficult days without the dog's companionship.

He also aimed to have a real heart-to-heart talk with Harvey, and thought it best to do so before they left Halfway.

Billy Joe opened the GMC's passenger side door, sat down, and begged Harvey's attention. "I lost my dog, my pride, and my mustache, all on the same day," he lamented. His voice cracked as he fought back tears. "I shouldn't have tried that stupid 'Billy Jack' routine. I took a beating for you, Harve. I got into a fight, and I deserved to get my ass whooped."

"No," argued Harvey. "No, you didn't deserve ..."

"I woulda gave me life for you, if that's what it took," interrupted Billy Joe. "Even if that dumb oaf had killed me, it woulda been worth it."

Harvey's mouth dropped open.

"I love you, Harve," said Billy Joe. "I love you more than anything! I don't care who knows it, or if people try to kill us over it. I love you."

Harvey tried to speak. It came out as a whimper.

"I don't care if I go to Hell for it," Billy Joe went on. "I love you, and want you as my one and only from now on. I want you with me when I go into the Army, and I want you with me as I ... as we head to Nashville and I make a name for myself in country music. I can't go on without you, and

I wouldn't care to try!"

Harvey mouthed I love you too, as tears streamed from his eyes.

"My grandparents know we're in love, and they're cool about it," informed Billy Joe. "Most of my aunts and uncles and cousins know too, and they don't give a hoot or a holler. If they do, they never said nothing to me about it. Some of our friends know, and they don't care neither. Hell, for all we know, pretty much everybody at Big W knows, and I don't give a damn what they gotta say over it!"

Fear grabbed Harvey like a vice.

"I took a beating for ya," said Billy Joe. "And I ain't a damn bit sorry for it. You willing to take a beating for me?"

"What makes you think I wouldn't?" Harvey blurted out, in the heat of the moment. "If you don't think I would, you don't know me half as much as you think ..."

"You gonna tell your folks about us? I ain't about to date you on a bootleg basis, where we gotta sneak around and hide it! I know you're scared, Harve, but I don't know what of."

Harvey gritted his teeth. He wanted to lash out, but lacked the ammunition.

"What're you scared of?" asked Billy Joe. "You scared of what your folks might say about us? Or are you scared of yourself?"

***

Harvey and Billy Joe fetched a few snacks from the Halfway Market for their trip home.

They didn't get far. Billy Joe tried to start the GMC. To his frustration, worry, and ill-humor, the rig experienced yet another vapor lock.

After several tries to start the engine, Billy Joe gave up. He stared blankly through the windshield and sighed. He mumbled a few cusswords under his breath and wondered what to do next.

"We gotta be at work tomorrow morning!" screamed Harvey.

"Don'tcha think I know that?" snapped Billy Joe, once again trying to rev the engine. It was no use. Each attempt led to failure, anxiety, anger, and even more cusswords.

"Now what?" mumbled Harvey, rolling his eyes back and sighing.

"Well, hell. There's gotta be a mechanic somewhere in this town. We'll get nowhere by just sitting here, feeling sorry for ourselves. Finding help's gotta be better than pissing and moaning."

With nothing else to do, Harvey and Billy Joe returned to the Halfway Market for assistance. They soon reached the counter of the hardware section, where a couple of male cashiers discussed baseball. "May I help you?" one of the cashiers asked.

Wearing a strained smile, Billy Joe explained that his pickup had a "bad case" of vapor lock, and if anyone was around to give it a look-see.

One of the cashiers, a fellow with a crew-cut and black, pencil-thin mustache, asked to help Harvey and Billy Joe out.

"Go for it," the other cashier said.

The fellow with the mustache fetched a John Deere cap and followed Harvey and Billy Joe to the GMC. He made pleasant conversation about guns, hunting, and fishing, as the trio 'meandered to the problem.'

"Hope ya don't mind me askin'," the mustache said, hesitantly, staring at the bandages wrapped around Billy Joe's noggin. "You mind tellin' me how you got so bunged up? Seems to me like you run head-first into a freight train."

Billy Joe rubbed his hand against the bandages as he fought back a giggle. "Aw, it ain't nothin'," he claimed, with a grin. "I walked right straight into a low-hanging branch the other day, up at Fish Lake."

"You mean to tell me a tree branch done that much damage?" the mustache questioned, in disbelief.

"I walked into it," Billy Joe mumbled, "eight or nine times ..."

"More like eight or nine dozen times," commented Harvey.

The mustache wrinkled his face, shook his head, and snickered.

"I wasn't watchin' what the hell I was doin'," Billy Joe went on. "And ... well ... you know how us shithead country boys are. We're our own worst enemies, we're never watchin' where we're goin', and we ain't got sense enough to pour piss outa a boot."

"You got that right!" the mustache laughed.

Once Billy Joe popped open the GMC's hood, the mustache removed the manifold and did a brief examination. After fooling with the carburetor, he asked Billy Joe to try the ignition.

Billy Joe did what was asked.

No luck.

"Try 'er again," the mustache suggested.

Once again, no success.

Harvey paced back and forth, checking the time on his cell phone. What good was that? The phone's battery was dead, and gave him nothing more than a blank screen and a panic attack.

"I hate to tell ya this," the mustache said, slamming the hood down, "but I'm thinkin' your carburetor's shot."

Billy Joe's eyes widened. Neither he or Harvey were mechanics, and couldn't dispute what the mustache told them. Both grew more tense with each passing word.

"I got me a Jimmy kinda like this, yonder, in my barn," the mustache explained, wiping grease from his hands. "Just a parts car, ya see. I can sell ya the carb off o' that, put 'er in your rig tonight, then getcha back on the road by ... Say ... First thing tomorrow mornin'?"

Harvey gave Billy Joe a look of desperation and despair.

"Well, now," the mustache said, sympathetically. "How 'bout it?"

"How much for the parts and labor?" asked Billy Joe, fearing the response.

"Oh, I dunno." The mustache smiled. "Couple hundred bucks?"

Billy Joe frowned.

"Well look it, buddy," the mustache said. "It's gonna be a damn sight cheaper than goin' out and buyin' a new carb, I'll tell ya that. Getcha back home, and I won't charge ya for the labor. Just the carb." The mustache laughed and pointed at Main Street Cafe. "'Less you wanna buy me a burger an' a Sprite, yonder. That, on account of you bein' a helluva nice guy. Right, buddy?"

Billy Joe sucked in a deep breath, then slowly shook the mustache's hand. "Deal," he said, with a mixture of reluctance and relief. "When you gonna make the repairs?"

"I get off work at six tonight," the mustache said. "Take your rig to my place, just a few miles out on Slaughterhouse Road. Put my carb in your rig, see if it works which I figure it just might, and getcha back on the road."

"Well?" asked Billy Joe, glancing at Harvey.

"We gotta be at work with the dawn patrol tomorrow!" Harvey whined, hopelessly.

Billy Joe smirked. "Dunno what else to do, Harve."

"What about our jobs?"

"That's not the only problem we got," mumbled Billy Joe, motioning toward the back where Corky remained wrapped in the sleeping bag.

Harvey gulped.

"I'll mosey on over to the bank and fetch you the money," Billy Joe told the mustache.

Harvey recalled the cash that the Subaru driver offered him earlier. He retrieved it from his wallet and handed it to the mustache. "Covered part of it," he said, in resignation.

The mustache chuckled and accepted the cash. "I'll getcha safely home. The name's Steele. Brent Steele. Nice Jimmy ya got here. See if I can make it even better, which I damn well might."

"Harvey Madden," the younger kid introduced, shaking Steele's hand.

"Billy Joe McBain, but you can call me ..." He sighed. "Aw, just call me ... Billy Joe."

Steele shoved the money in his jeans pocket. "I gotta get back to work. If ya want, meet me yonder, buy me the Sprite and a burger t' go. I'll tow your Jimmy to my barn, and have it up and runnin' before ya know it."

"Much obliged," acknowledged Billy Joe.

As Steele returned to the Halfway Market, Harvey and Billy Joe stayed behind to contemplate their situation.

Billy Joe was in no big rush to push carts that next day, yet wondered where he might spend the night. He only hoped to make the most out of a mess and keep smiling.

On the other hand, Harvey wanted to get home. Sure, it was great to get away from Big W and spend a few days in the mountains. He'd always appreciate the love, support, and companionship he got from the Tanakas and Derrys. He'd forever value the bike that Cliff Walker gave him. He'd treasure the night he made love to Billy Joe under the stars. It sickened him to learn that Dani (of all people!) had eavesdropped on the most private of matters. He'd never cease to detest her over that!

And although Harvey disliked Corky, he never wished to see the dog die in such a way.

More than anything, Harvey craved the comfort and security of home. He'd take a long, hot shower, get into clean clothes, then watch a bit of TV or listen to music.

There was also a more pressing concern which Harvey hoped to avoid. He had no choice but to face it, if he wished to maintain a relationship with Billy Joe. If Harvey had plans of being totally honest with himself, didn't it also mean coming out, and coming clean, to two of the most important people in his life? ...

Terry and Elaine Madden?

Eventually, Terry and Elaine were likely to gain the truth, if they didn't already harbor suspicions. Wasn't it best for them to hear it from Harvey, and not someone else?

So, how would Harvey's folks handle it? Would they be happy, sad, shocked, outraged, or in denial? Would they show Harvey the door, where he'd fend for himself in a cold, cruel world?

"Well," whined Harvey. "What're we gonna do now?"

"First thing we gotta do is take care of Corky," spoke Billy Joe, sadly.

Harvey leaned against the GMC's passenger door. Maybe he'd lose his job at Big W. He was determined never to lose the boy, standing a mere few feet away. A boy who now mourned the loss of a dog. No matter what, Harvey would never, could never, abide thoughts of losing the most precious of commodities …

The possibilities of spending his life without the one he loved so dearly …

Billy Joe McBain.

28

Harvey and Billy Joe took time to conceal particular items throughout the GMC. Billy Joe's rifle, shotgun, and pistol were covered under
blankets behind the cab's seat. Coolers filled with beer were placed on the
floorboard, and the cab locked up.

Billy Joe located Cliff's number in the phone book at the Main Street
Cafe. He hoped the old man would find a suitable place to bury Corky and,
if necessary, offer a couch or spare bed to crash on.

Meanwhile, Harvey sought moments of solitude. He needed to clear
his head, and be alone. His thoughts were muddled, his mind filled with
confusion, anxiety, fear, and pain. Everything seemingly fell apart that
morning. Corky's death, Billy Joe's rage, the brawl with Dani and that big
ape, and finally the vapor lock. Harvey expected something else to go to
haywire before another hour passed.

Harvey had gotten his cell phone charged at the cafe. Later, he wandered to the Lions Club Park, to get his thoughts together. He told Billy
Joe to call him, once he had contacted Cliff and hopefully arranged lodgings.

Harvey sat alone at a bench in the park, drinking a Coke and praying
he wouldn't lose his job or his mind. While he didn't always like being a
cashier, it was money in his pocket and the assurance of a paycheck every
other Thursday. For the most part, Big W had actually treated him well,
and he felt like part of one big family.

In time, Harvey figured he'd have to come out to Terry and Elaine.

He hesitated, fearing it'd shatter any level of love and affection they held toward him. How else might Terry and Elaine feel knowing that Harvey would never find a girl to call his own, or give them more biological grandchildren to spoil? The idea that Harvey offered them a son-in-law, and not a daughter-in-law, would obviously affect them ... but how?

And while Billy Joe was a good guy, at least in Harvey's opinion, he didn't exactly fit into the Madden clan. Terry and Elaine were committed, die-hard liberal Democrats, and insisted their kids believed in a similar fashion. What was Billy Joe? A rough-hewn cowboy, not very sophisticated or well-educated, and raised by Republican grandparents. Billy Joe planned to become a proud member of the Grand Old Party and a champion of conservative causes, such as the right to bear arms while adopting a pro-life agenda.

Rarely did Harvey agree with Billy Joe on politics. The two still had each other. Even then, Harvey loathed and feared Billy Joe's plans of joining the Army. No matter. Harvey and Billy Joe were destined to have their differences. And, somehow, maybe they'd learn to work them out, accept them, and continue to care for each other.

It was impossible for Harvey to conceal his love for Billy Joe, especially if marriage entered the equation. Well, damn it! Terry and Elaine had to know the truth, and Harvey had to be the one to give it to them.

Right?

Right?

Once more, panic gripped Harvey. There was nothing he could do about it. Maybe the only way to free himself from such fear was to get everything out in the open, and let his parents come to terms of having a gay son.

"I hoped to find you," someone spoke from behind. "And here's exactly where I thought to find you!"

Harvey turned around and saw Debra stepping toward him. He inadvertently let out a hysterical giggle. Although he preferred being alone, Harvey knew that talking to another person was better than talking to himself. If he remained alone for too long, he might very well go insane. And he wasn't far from it, anyway.

Harvey invited Debra to sit with him on the bench. "I thought maybe you had already left."

"I thought about it," said Debra. "I just wanted to make sure you were okay."

"I'm all right, no thanks to Dani. So where is she?"

"I don't know, and I don't care."

Harvey sought illumination.

"I heard about what Dani and that Neanderthal did to you and Billy Joe this morning ... And last night," explained Debra. "She got back to our hotel room, carrying on about what ... What she saw, and told me what she had in mind for you and Billy Joe. Kept saying she was 'gonna let you have it'."

"Yeah," said Harvey, "and we 'got it', too."

"I want nothing more to do with Dani. She might be my cousin. It doesn't mean we gotta be friends. If Dani wants to spend her life being a hag, it doesn't mean I have to go along with it."

"Has she always been that way?"

Debra nodded, 'yes'. "Her whole family's like her. Mom, dad, brothers and sisters. All pissed off and miserable. They claim to hate minorities, which is strange considering they don't really know any."

Harvey rolled his eyes back and sighed.

"It only got worse when Dani had to compete with this black chick in high school," Debra went on. "Allison Washington, from Joseph. The two usually went up against each other in cross country or track and field. Oh, yeah. Volleyball and basketball, too." Debra grinned. "What can I say about Allison? She's really smart and talented. She's got the body of a gazelle and the speed of a jaguar. Smart, charming, athletic, funny, and gorgeous as hell. And I mean ... gorgeous as hell."

"Okay."

"No matter how hard Dani tried," continued Debra, "she could never beat Allison in the hundred-meter dash, pole vault, or anything else. It only added to Dani's resentment toward her. It never paid for Allison to try and have a conversation with Dani. Dani always ended up screaming racial slurs at her."

Harvey nodded, 'yes'.

"Allison got a huge scholarship to attend USC," added Debra. "I can only guess where that might take her."

"What about Dani?" pondered Harvey.

"I doubt if she'll ever leave Elgin. Probably marry some pissed off, drunken bum like her old man, have a bunch of mean, ugly kids, live in a trailer park, and become even more miserable than she already is."

Harvey and Debra shared a laugh.

"I just wanted to see you before I left," said Debra. "I was worried, and had to make sure you were okay."

"Are you going back today?" asked Harvey, nervously.

"Yeah. Why?"

Harvey explained that the GMC had broken down, and wouldn't be on the road until the day after. He had to be at work by that next morning, and asked to bum a ride.

"Sure!" agreed Debra, excitedly. "I'd love to have you come with me!"

Harvey shook Debra's hand. He fetched his cell phone, called Billy Joe, and informed him he'd travel to Grangeford with her.

Billy Joe had managed to secure lodgings that evening with Cliff. The old man agreed to help bury Corky under an apricot tree in a secluded space near Homestead, Oregon, on the Snake River. Later, Cliff and Billy Joe would go to the mountains to tell lies about fishing and hunting, then shoot off a few rounds in target practice.

Harvey got off the phone, took a deep breath, then let it out in a sigh. He wiped sweat from his forehead, got to both feet, and straightened his aching back. "Well, I guess that does it, then," he said to Debra, in relief. "Looks like I'm going with you. Just lemme get a few things from the rig, and we'll be on our way."

"Just a moment," Debra spoke, urgently. Slowly, she reached out to place Harvey's hand in hers, and gave it a tight squeeze. She was reluctant to get her feelings out. "I ... I don't think there's a chance you might forgot all about ... Billy Joe, and let me to be your Cinderella, and for you to be my ... my Prince Charming." Debra bit her bottom lip. "Is there?"

Harvey frowned. "I'm sorry, Debra, but I've already got my 'Prince Charming'. Like I said, I'm his Prince Charming, which makes him mine."

Debra's face altered to a fiery blush. "You think? ... You think I'll ever find my Prince Charming?" she whispered. "You think he's out there ... Waiting for me, somewhere?"

"A sweet girl like you?" Harvey laughed. "Of course, he's out there! You'll know it when you find him, and if you're as smart as I think you are, you'll never let him go, not for all the riches in the world! Trust me! I got my Prince Charming and, for what it's worth, some happy day you'll have yours!"

***

Harvey returned to the GMC to find Billy Joe waiting for him. Billy Joe removed some of Harvey's personal things from the cab and placed them on the sidewalk. "Looks like you'll keep your job at Big W, after all," he said, sarcastically. "They're gonna have a helluva time keeping up with carts while I'm gone, but I reckon they'll just have to get by without me."

"Want me to call you as soon as I get home?" asked Harvey.

"Aw, if ya want to." Billy Joe frowned. "Gonna miss not having you with me. But, knowing that macho, tough guy things like guns and hunting ain't your thing, reckon it's just as well."

Harvey slouched. Yeah, part on him wished to stay with Billy Joe. Yet, he was obliged in returning to Grangeford. Not only did he have a job to go to, but also a private matter with his parents. That was, if he had to courage to go through with it. "Try not to brag yourself up too much around Cliff," he said. "There might be two graves under an apricot tree in Homestead, and not just one."

"That reminds me." Billy Joe leaned against the GMC as he rubbed the bandages covering his injured forehead. "Cliff knows I threw the trap shoot yesterday."

Harvey's mouth dropped open. "How'd he find out?"

"Said I made it look too obvious," explained Billy Joe. "Said I deliberately missed a shot that any half-wit or blind man could hit. He wanted to whoop me, fair and square, and it was only a matter of time before he got around to it. Said if I pulled that kinda stunt again he'd kick my ass till my nose bled. So, I told him it was your idea, and now he's gonna kick your ass till your nose bleeds, too."

Harvey searched for the right thing to say. The best he could do was to mumble, "Well ..." and leave it at that.

"You sure you don't wanna stay here with me when I say my goodbyes to Corky?" requested Billy Joe. His emotions nearly got the better of him. "Sure you and Debra can't hang around long enough for when I say words over him?"

Harvey felt a certain responsibility or what happened to Corky. But he never liked the dog, and wasn't up to pretending that he ever did. He felt badly for Billy Joe, but would never miss Corky ... Not one bit. He figured that Billy Joe was liable to find another dog, and only hoped it wasn't as mean-spirited, unpredictable, and jealous as Corky.

"I love you," said Harvey, embracing Billy Joe.

Billy Joe held onto Harvey, as tight as he could. Although he tried holding it back, he couldn't prevent a teardrop or two from leaving the eyes. "I love you, too," he breathed. "You're the best thing that ever happened to me."

"The same for you. I dunno how I got so lucky to have you in my life. But now that I'm yours, and you're mine, no one's getting between us."

"You never gave me an answer for what I asked you earlier." Billy Joe took a deep breath. "And I want your answer, now."

Harvey glanced at Billy Joe, in confusion.

"Will you marry me?" Billy Joe's throat tightened. He struggled to present the question, once more. It came out as simply being mouthed.

Will you marry me?

Harvey tried but failed to conceal his own tears. Unable to give a verbal response, he answered the only way he knew how.

Not caring of who saw it, and not really caring what others might have thought, Harvey gave his own private, redneck Prince Charming yet another hug.

This time, however, he kissed Billy Joe on the lips.

29

Elaine Madden had spent the morning doing housework. By eleven, she had completed most chores, then took time to sit down on her favorite recliner and put her feet up. She was dressed in a light blue, long-sleeved blouse, modest shorts, and leather sandals. She found the remote to a sixty-five-inch Samsung TV in the family room and channel surfed.

To Elaine's delight, David Lean's version of 'Doctor Zhivago' was on TCM. Elaine sprinted to the kitchen for a can of beer and a bag of organic corn chips. She returned to the recliner and pigged out, a celebration with herself as the sole party-goer.

An hour into the movie, Elaine heard a vehicle stop in front of the house. A car door opened, then slammed shut. The car speeded away, and seconds later Harvey wandered into the house. He carried a backpack over one shoulder and was dog-tired.

Elaine hopped from the recliner, ran to the door, and greeted Harvey with a kiss on the cheek.

"Nice to see you, Mom," yawned Harvey, feeling like he might collapse at any moment. He dropped the pack next to a couch, hugged Elaine, then asked where Terry was.

"On his afternoon ritual," said Elaine, referring to Terry's daily walk around the city of Grangeford, a distance of nearly twelve miles. It was a route which Terry followed since semi-retiring a few years back, a means of staying in shape. While a few pals had tried to accompany Terry on these hikes, few managed to keep up. No matter. Terry preferred to walk alone so he'd never be bothered by annoying and needless chatter.

Harvey had planned to sit down with his parents, once he got home. He wished to do so, immediately, before cold feet stopped him. During the trip from Halfway to Grangeford, Harvey had rehearsed a speech in his own mind, and prayed he had it down. Whether it was memorized or not he still had to present it for real ... Then forever deal with its consequences.

"What do you want to see your father about?" inquired Elaine, falling back on her old habit of expecting bad news.

Harvey wondered if it wasn't best to first talk to Elaine, and then Terry. By now, a near-crippling anxiety took hold.

Harvey simply smiled. He needed to take a shower, change his clothes, and enjoy a brief nap. He retreated upstairs to his bedroom, thinking himself a coward for lacking the ability to have a heart-to-heart with Elaine.

He still had the opportunity ...

Didn't he?

Harvey entered his room and hastily removed his sweaty clothes. He eagerly ran into a bathroom next to his quarters. There, he took a hot shower and gave himself the chance to relax and get his thoughts together.

Whether he was prepared to chat with Terry and Elaine, Harvey continued going over and over it in his mind. He couldn't keep his heart from racing out of control. Panic engulfed him.

Harvey got out of the shower and dried off. He glanced at his scrawny, nude frame in a full-sized mirror, nailed to a closet door. He took a deep breath. The only obstacle standing in his way was himself ... along with extreme fear and a wild imagination.

Harvey thought about what Angela had told him, in the safe confines of a tent at Fish Lake.

You believe it is a secret, but it never really has been.

Whether Harvey's sexuality was a secret or not, soon it wouldn't be ... If only he gave himself permission to spit it out.

Harvey dressed in a Grangeford High sweatshirt, a pair of tan cargo shorts, and worn-out sneakers. He reached into a small, dorm fridge in the corner of his bedroom for a can of beer, and sought courage from it.

Well, the first beer tasted so good, why not have another?

After downing a third brew, Harvey went into the bathroom to relieve himself. He sucked in a couple of breaths, straightened his spine, and wandered downstairs to handle important business.

Harvey blundered to the family room, feeling light and loose on his own feet. Intoxication mixed with fraying nerves. Harvey questioned whether he'd laugh through his chat with Terry and Elaine, or vomit upon the kitchen table once he opened his mouth.

Elaine remained in her favorite recliner until 'Doctor Zhivago' neared its climax. Harvey sat on the couch, wrestling with himself on whether or not to make a necessary revelation.

Once the end credits and the memorable Maurice Jarre filled the screen, Harvey reluctantly asked to have Terry and Elaine speak with him in the dining room.

"What's up, honey?" questioned Elaine. "Anything wrong?"

"Please, Mom?" begged Harvey, in a jittery voice. He motioned toward the dining room. "May I speak with you and Dad?"

Elaine shut off the TV, then quickly went to fetch Terry from the study.

Harvey entered the dining room. His legs were like spaghetti. Both hands were covered in sweat. He sat at the table, contemplating on what to say and how to say it. From the study, he heard Terry arguing politics and religion with a former Asian-American coworker. Nervous laughter escaped from Harvey's mouth. He wondered if he faced a new beginning, or the beginning of the end, or the end of the beginning.

For what seemed like an eternity, Harvey waited until Terry and Elaine entered the dining room. Elaine wore expressions of deep worry, which always got the worst of her. Terry was high on marijuana, and exceedingly peeved about a heated exchange with Henry Kuwahara over a spending bill being considered by the Oregon Senate. He traded glances with Harvey, as a comical smile highlighted his face. Terry slapped Harvey's shoulder, and asked if the lad had a good trip.

"Okay," mouthed Harvey. He pointed at a chair next to him, and directed Terry to sit down.

Without asking why, Terry did as he was told. Meanwhile, Elaine stood at the kitchen sink and expected the worst.

"Please, Mom?" begged Harvey.

"What? ... What is it, honey?" whined Elaine. "Is it about? ... Billy Joe? Is he? ... He didn't accidentally shoot somebody ... did he?"

"He's all right," mumbled Harvey, his voice barely audible. This was the moment of truth, a point where he'd enter a reality from which there was no going back. "Please, Mom?" he repeated, once again pointing at the chair.

Elaine stared at Harvey, while Terry first smirked then openly chuckled at these mysterious proceedings.

Harvey took a deep breath. His eyes first fixated on the faded, checkered table cloth, and away from his parents.

This is it ...

This is where life changes ...

Well, there was no need to explain himself, or struggle with words to uphold and defend his affections and devotion to Billy Joe. Better to get it out now, without stuttering over heartfelt pleas for understanding, forgiveness, and love. Still, no matter what he did to prevent it, Harvey couldn't keep his face from altering to a fiery blush. Nor could he hold back the tears from running down his face. His throat tightened, and voice grew increasingly high-pitched and raspy.

Harvey reached out to take Terry and Elaine's hands. He forced himself to make eye-contact with them as he made his next, gutsy move.

"Mom ... Dad ..." he uttered, in a sob. "I'm gay."

THE END

ABOUT THE AUTHOR

Doug McKim has worked as a dishwasher, a janitor, a journalist, a prep cook, a deli clerk, a mentor, a tutor, a volunteer for economic and community development, a caregiver, and a grave digger. He has a degree in History from Eastern Oregon University.

Originally from Halfway, Oregon, McKim spent a year in Tennessee before settling in La Grande. He is the author of five books: ARE YOU MAN ENOUGH (2010, co-authored with Richard McKim), JUST PLAIN OLD JEREMY (2012), ONE DAY IN THE LIFE OF MARTY McKENNA (2013), LOVE, DEATH, AND ART (2017), and HARVEY MADDEN (2022).

*Visit the author's website at **dougmckim.com** to learn more about his novels, where to buy them, and get the latest news.*